The Willberry Inn

An Oak Harbor Series

Kimberly Thomas

Prologue

Six months ago

Cora turned to the door as it creaked open. She stood facing her husband as he stepped fully into the room. His suit jacket and tie were gone, the first two buttons of his shirt were undone, and the sleeves were rolled up to his forearms. His chestnut-colored hair was messy as if he had been running his fingers through it.

He looked at her with a mixture of surprise and panic. Evidently, he had spent the hour downstairs hoping she would already be asleep by the time he came up.

The two stood facing each other, neither one saying a word. Joel sighed, his shoulders sagging in defeat.

"Cor—"

"Who is she?" Cora demanded before he could finish.

Joel's eyes widened in surprise, lips parted. Recovering from the initial shock, he asked, "What are you talking about?"

Joel's feeble attempt to appear ignorant only served to elevate her anger.

"Don't play this game with me, Joel," she seethed. Squaring her shoulders and narrowing her eyes into tiny slits, she pushed, "Who are you having an affair with?"

"Cora." He breathed out exhaustedly, running his long fingers through his already disheveled hair. "Cora, I'm not having an affair. I love you." His tone was even, eyes pleading.

At his declaration, Cora scoffed in disbelief. "You love me?" Her chest heaved as she tried to control the angry tears that wanted to fall. "You love me," she echoed it again slowly, trying to make the words make sense to her as she looked past him. "How can you use those words so loosely, Joel?" she asked, her head shaking back and forth. This time, the tears fell unhindered. Fixing her teary eyes on him, she continued, "You barely touch me anymore. You don't even kiss me good morning like you used to or make an effort for us to have breakfast together in the mornings."

Joel gulped and looked down guiltily as she listed the things he had stopped doing.

"Tonight was my night. You knew how special that journalism award was to me," she continued as her anger overshadowed the pain she was feeling.

"I'm so sorry, honey. I know I messed up—"

"You were on your phone the entire ceremony," she screeched, throwing her hands up in frustration. "You're always on your phone. At god-awful hours of the night when you should be asleep, you're up on that wretched device." After a short pause, she looked him in the eye. "I stood on that stage, waiting for you to look at me— to acknowledge my accomplishment," she sobbed. "Then we come home, and you stay downstairs without even trying to make an effort to see why I was so upset—"

"Cora," he pleaded, reaching his hand out to touch her.

"Don't... don't touch me," she warned. She didn't need his touch. She didn't want his sudden attempt at affection. Not now— not when she needed the truth from him. His hand immediately fell to his side.

"I have wanted you to touch me the way you used to for the past six months, to kiss me like I'm the only woman who matters to you. Instead, what did I get? A husband who comes home late at night yet stays up watching television, waiting for me to fall asleep so he can come to bed." Cora shook her head, then continued. "I can only assume that you're cheating on me." She spoke with resignation as she raised her red eyes to stare into those of her husband's, daring him to lie to her one more time. "Who is she?"

"I swear, Cora, I am not cheating on you. There is no one else," Joel proclaimed, his moss-green eyes willing her to believe him. "I love you. I promise. I am not cheating."

When she didn't reply, he fell to his knees and earnestly grabbed her hands between his own, disregarding her earlier warning. "I swear, Cora. You are the love of my life. There is no one else," he pleaded.

Cora looked down at her husband, at the wetness gathering at the corners of his eyes. He still had her heart. Still, something held her back from accepting his words. Taking her hands from his grasp, she turned away from him.

"Cora." She heard him say as he shuffled to his feet.

"I, I just need some time to think," she threw over her shoulder as she headed for the closet adjacent to the bedroom door. Pulling out her running gear and shoes, she quickly stepped out of her robe and donned her outfit.

She turned to see Joel watching her helplessly, shoulders slouched.

"I'm going for a run," she explained. "I just need some time to think, and I can't do it here. Maybe when I get back, we can talk about what is really going on then?"

Joel eagerly nodded. "Sure, okay," he agreed, giving her a small smile. He looked as if he wanted to say more but held himself back. Without another word, she walked past him, made her way downstairs, and slipped through the front door.

After Cora warmed up, she took off down the road in a sprint, feeling the cool air wash over her. She maintained a steady rhythm as her body moved farther away from her home. Her heart pounded within her chest, keeping count with her feet hitting the pavement as the cool night air caressed her face and dried the tiny beads of sweat that formed on her brows from how hard she was running.

Running was one of her favorite pastimes. The thrilling experience kept her athletic body in shape and youthful. She loved anything that had to do with the outdoors and challenged her physically. Tonight, she ran for another reason; her marriage was on the rocks, and she didn't know how to fix it. She loved being a problem solver, but this was getting the best of her.

One thing she was relieved about was that Joel wasn't cheating on her. He said there was no one else. He seemed so sincere. She wanted to believe him, but she couldn't knock the foreboding feeling deep within her gut. But she wanted her marriage—she still loved him—and she couldn't fathom twenty-three years of spending her life as Joel's wife ending like this. Slowing her pace until she came to a halt, she bent over with her palms on her knees, panting to catch her breath.

Her mind continued to play over all that happened before she left the house. No solution came to mind, but as she straightened herself, she concluded that she would fight for her marriage.

Just as she turned in the direction of her house, her cell phone rang.

"Hello?"

"Hi, Cora, it...it's Samantha. Are you home?"

The apprehension in her best friend's voice put Cora on high alert.

"I'm not. What's wrong, Sam? You sound upset. Are you by the house? I'm on my way back now," she rushed out, speed-walking down the sidewalk.

"No. I'm fine. It's just... I-I'm not sure how to say this."

Cora's pace slowed as she waited for Samantha to continue.

"Sam. What is it? Tell me, please." Cora was full-on panicking.

"I'm so sorry to break it to you like this, Cora, but you need to know before the scandal reaches your doorstep."

Her heart clenched with anxiety. She stopped walking and rested her free hand against one of the many trees lining the sidewalk.

"You know how you had a feeling Joel was having an affair?" Sam asked.

"Yes, I confronted him tonight, and he swore he wasn't," she hurried to say.

"Cora." Whenever Samantha's voice took on a note of sympathy, she always knew it would be something that would affect her deeply.

"I knew it would be hard to tell you this, but I underestimated how hard it would be." Samantha sighed.

Cora waited, pressing more of her weight onto the tree for whatever support she would need after Sam's revelation.

"Joel is being investigated by the Ophthalmology Disciplinary Tribunal for misconduct in the workplace. Chances are he could lose his license."

"What are you talking about? What kind of misconduct, Sam?" Cora asked, needing her to say the words that could mean the end of her marriage or the end of any plans to work through their problems.

"He is being investigated for using company resources to pursue a licentious relationship with one of his patients."

Cora felt her heart finally shatter as she slid to the ground, still holding the phone tightly to her ear. She couldn't believe Joel had looked her in the eye and lied so easily. She wished the ground would open at that moment and suck her into its dark recesses.

"Do... Do you have a name?" she choked out.

"I'm sorry, Cora. I wish I could give you a name, but I can't in my position as chair of the committee. As your friend, what I can say is... it's someone you trusted with the care of your home and your family."

Cora leaned against the tree as her head spun with the information. She felt dizzy and light-headed.

"Are you still there?"

"Yes... Yes, I'm here. I'm just. I don't know..." Cora's voice came out barely above a whisper.

"Where are you? Let me get you. Maybe it's better not to go back home tonight," Samantha offered.

"No. It's fine... I need to get this over with. Thanks, Sam. I know you didn't have to tell me, but I'm grateful."

She heard her friend's heavy sigh through her phone. "Cora, you're my best friend. There is no way I would let you get blindsided by this news, Chair or not."

Cora was grateful for her friend. She was one of the few people she could count on to be there for her, and she was appreciative of their friendship.

"Thanks, Sam. I gotta go."

"Call me," Sam replied before the call ended.

"I will," she promised.

After about ten minutes of sitting with her back braced up against the tree, Cora found the strength to get up and start back home. She wasn't sure what she would say to Joel when she finally faced him, but Cora knew this was it for her— she was done. She felt completely numb.

"Hey, you're back. How was your run?" Joel asked as soon as she came through the front door. "Cora?"

Cora fixed her eyes on him. She wasn't sure what he saw in them, but his sharp intake of breath and subtle step back meant he knew something was about to happen.

"You've been having an affair with Cindy?" The calmness of her voice surprised her as much as the question shook her husband.

"Cor-Cora." His voice quivered. His eyes reflected his guilt.

"Seriously?"

"Cora, please let me expl— "

Cora's palm connected hard with Joel's cheek, mid-sentence. The harsh slap of her hand against his skin echoed in the now silent room. Her palm stung from the blow, but she didn't care. She wanted him to shut up.

"Right under my nose. I can't believe this." She wanted to hit him again for making such a fool out of her, to find the heaviest object in the room to bludgeon him with. Instead, she began pacing back and forth frantically to suppress the impulse.

Finally, she stopped and let out a humorless laugh.

"You and our housekeeper... It's quite funny, you know." Cora shook her head.

"You were so adamant that we not hire her, and in the end, you do this. I've got to tell you, Joel, you had everyone fooled, especially me. I thought you two didn't quite click. I guess that was just a show for me, right? To throw me off?" Cora put her hands together, applauding. "Congratulations!"

"Cor—"

Cora held her hand up, stopping him from continuing.

"How long?"

She didn't think Joel's eyes could get any wider than they already were, yet it seemed they grew at her question.

"Um, uh, well....um... one year." Joel hung his head in defeat.

"Well, I was way off. I predicted six months or seven tops, but this has been going on for a whole year," she spat incredulously.

"Cora, I'm sorry, I—"

"Not as sorry as you're going to be." She cut him off. "We had a family with twenty-three years of marriage. We built an entire life together, and you threw that all away so easily. What about our girls? What am I supposed to tell them?"

"I'm sorry, Cora. I didn't mean for this to happen. I love you. I want us. I will do better, I promise. I won't do it again. Please."

"You're right. You won't do it again because there won't be a next time. I want you out of this house."

"Cora, please, I—"

"I don't care where you go. Just don't be here when I get back."

With that, Cora turned around and walked right back through the front door, leaving her husband standing there in disbelief.

Chapter One

"Mr. Avlon has agreed to let you keep the family home, and all the items contained there."

Cora nodded in understanding as her lawyer went through the terms of the divorce document. It had been six months since she kicked her lying, cheating husband out of the home they had shared for over seventeen years of their twenty-three-year marriage.

She remembered when they decided to move from their old apartment, so they could have more space, and their growing girls could have their own rooms. Joel's practice was picking up, and she was an up-and-coming journalist, already known for her factual pieces and ability to get interviews with high-profile celebrities who would normally shun the media. They were both raking in enough cash for them to purchase their own home. A home she thought they would live in until they were old. She had imagined they would welcome their girls with their own families here for visits. She had imagined the feet of their many grandchildren running up and down the stairs while she and Joel tried their best to chase them. She had not envisioned this at all.

Soon the divorce would be complete, and she would start picking up the remaining pieces of her life to start over alone.

"What about the beach house in Panama City?" she asked.

Her lawyer sifted through the pages of the settlement agreement, seeking information about the property.

"Ah... here it is. It says he is seeking full ownership of the property but is willing to negotiate for part ownership." Her lawyer looked expectantly over his glasses as he waited for her reply.

"He can have it." She wanted everything split down the middle or as close as they could get. Anything else just wouldn't do.

She didn't want to own anything with him. She hadn't even spoken to him in the past four months. Even when he had reached out to her, trying to explain or to apologize, she had turned a deaf ear to him. He'd been in a relationship with their housekeeper for an entire year. There was no going back after that.

Even the girls had cut him out of their lives when they learned of the betrayal. She didn't want them to end their relationship with their father. He had been an exceptional father—she could not fault him on that—but they were hurting like she was.

* * *

Cora could still remember the calls she'd gotten from the girls a week after finding out about the affair. He had called and told them.

She had been sitting in the den, reminiscing about all the beautiful memories they'd made as a family in this house and how they used to crowd onto the couch that was only meant to seat three comfortably. At the same time, they ate their popcorn and watched the latest action shows and Hallmark movies. There were two other armchairs and an added loveseat in the room that no one ever made a move to sit on when they had family time. They loved being close to each other on this couch with the peeling leather. This piece of furniture by itself held so many memories for her.

Every year, they used to take their gifts from under the Christmas tree, pile them on the coffee table while they all sat on the couch, and take turns opening them. They had custom-made pajamas—elf ones for the girls, while she and Joel would be dressed in the Mr. and Mrs. Claus ones. Right after opening their gifts, they would snuggle on said couch, drinking hot cocoa and watching all of the *Home Alone* specials.

Tears streamed down her cheeks as she looked through the photo albums. She looked at how happy they had been— so in love that it manifested on the other side of the lens, captured for the world to see.

Cora stared at the photos of Joel at the births of their girls. The love and pride she saw there each time he held their girls immediately after their birth, the pictures of him kissing her temple with so much tenderness as she lay on the bed looking drained pulled at her heart. The love was so palpable— that wasn't something you could fake. But gradually, that love dwindled, and all that was left were the memories of what was and the fresh ones of a deception that cut so deep.

While looking through this album and occasionally sipping on the wine she had poured herself, her phone rang.

"Hello?"

"M-Mo...Mom..."

Erin's wobbly voice pouring through the speaker of her

phone caused Cora's heart to constrict with grief for her suffering.

"How could... how could Dad do this, Mom?" her daughter cried.

"I don't know, sweetie," she replied truthfully. She still hadn't been able to figure out why Joel felt the need to step outside of their marriage— not that she wanted to hear his reasons now.

"I want you to know it'll be okay, sweetie. I don't want you to worry about this. You—"

"How can you say that, Mom? Dad cheated on you. He deliberately hurt you, broke your trust and our family," Erin spoke through her tears.

Cora's tears started to fall as well, listening to her daughter's brokenness. What could she say to that? She knew it wouldn't all be okay, but she needed to be strong for them... for her girls.

"How could he do something so despicable and for so long?"

Cora could sense the shift in her daughter's emotions. She was angry now. Understandably. She had gone through a range of emotions since finding out the news. Emotions she never thought she would recover from.

"Erin, I know you're hurting, but he's your father, and no matter what happens between us, you need to know he loves you," Cora tried to appease her daughter.

"Well, that's his problem," she seethed. "I'm never speaking to him ever again."

"Erin—"

"No, Mom, I mean it. I'm never speaking to Dad again. He hurt you so much, and I can't forgive him for that. Even worse, it was with Cindy— of all people!" Erin exclaimed.

Cora sighed in defeat. She knew Erin was headstrong, so it made no sense to argue with her or try to get her to do what she didn't want to do. She reminded Cora so much of herself. She knew in time, Erin would be able to forgive her father, and though she knew the relationship wouldn't go back to what it was, it was best not to interfere but give her time to process it all.

"My sweet, sweet Erin... what would I do without you?" Cora asked hoarsely. "I love you and your sister so much. I wish I could shield you both from it all, but I'm happy that you have each other. Don't ever let anything break that bond. You're stronger together," she implored her firstborn. As she spoke, her mind flashed to her own siblings, and she felt a pang of regret.

"I won't, Mom. I promise... I love you."

Cora smiled, reassured that her girls would be okay.

"So, how is that handsome son-in-law of mine?" Cora asked, wanting to shift the conversation to something much more promising.

"Brian is fine, Mom. I told you to stop calling him that," Erin chided.

"Erin, you've been with him for five years now. In some countries, that is considered a lifelong commitment."

"Well, this is America, and we're still young. Anything is possible."

The ambiguity of the statement concerned Cora.

"Is everything okay with you guys?"

"Yeah, Mom, we're fine. I just don't... I don't know if we're meant to last, that's all," she answered truthfully.

Cora wondered if the events of her father's infidelity played a role in Erin's perspective on her relationship. Or maybe her daughter had been thinking about this for some time now. At any rate, she only wanted what was best for her child.

"Erin, if you're not sure, that's fine. Take your time. You're still young. If it's meant to last with Brian, it will, but whatever decision you make, you know you'll always have my support, sweetie."

"Thanks, Mom," Erin replied gratefully.

"I'm working on a project for work and preparing for my finals, but as soon as I have these cleared, I'll take some time off and come home."

"Oh, sweetie, you don't have to do that. I'm fine, I promise."

"No, Mom, I'm coming home. I want to, and it's fine. Besides, I miss you."

"Oh, sweetie, I miss you so much too. I'll see you then. I love you."

"Love you too, Mom. See you soon."

Shortly after her call with Erin, Julia called. After ranting on about how selfish her father was, her final resolve, like her sister, was that she would never forgive him.

"As far as I'm concerned, he's dead to me," Julia had said.

Like Erin, Cora knew Julia also needed time to process all that had happened before she would be ready to start mending her relationship with her father.

Sitting there in the lawyer's office, she couldn't believe six months had already passed, and with the divorce being finalized, it was like opening up a wound that had already started to heal as she sat across from him. She was eager for the divorce to be completed and this chapter of her life to be done with.

"He asks that the RV remain with him as it is his current home address." Another request she didn't have a problem complying with.

As much as she hated Joel for what he had done to her, she understood the plight he was in. He had lost his license, his practice, and all the perks of the position. The divorce wasn't cheap either. She would let him have it. It had been his anyway, as was the beach house.

They had inherited property—passed down to him upon

his father's death—along with a considerable sum of cash, which had allowed them to be more comfortable than they could have ever dreamed. They had been able to pay off the mortgage on their home, and both of their girls had gone on to college without having to take out student loans. The properties, therefore, were his, and she wasn't going to be petty.

"In the matter of alimony, how do you wish to proceed?"

She had thought about this carefully, and only one solution made the most sense to her.

"I would like a single lump-sum payment," she expressed.

Pausing from going through the document before him, Mr. Pike looked up at her.

"Mrs. Avlon," he started with apprehension. "Are you sure that is a wise idea?"

"I am," she assured him. She meant it when she said she wanted nothing to connect her and Joel anymore.

"Okay, I will add those terms."

Just as Mr. Pike finished, her phone rang. Looking down at the caller ID, she recognized it was her mother.

"Hello? Mom?"

"Cora..." Her mother's voice was barely above a whisper. This put Cora on edge.

"It's your dad," her mother sobbed.

Her heart fell to the floor of her stomach.

"Mom, what's wrong with Dad?" Cora managed to get out.

"He—" Her mother could barely contain herself.

"Mom... please, what happened," Cora asked as her mother cried uncontrollably into the phone.

After a few tries at speaking up, her mother finally said the words Cora had not expected to hear, not so soon.

"Cora, your dad, he was in a car accident, and well... th-they rushed him to the hospital, but Cora, he didn't make it. My Samuel. He's gone." At this, her mother broke down again.

Cora sat in the chair unmoving, unable to process the news that her father was dead.

Cora noticed Mr. Pike looking at her, his face marred with worry. He must have recognized something was not right the moment her hand gripped her phone, and all the color drained from her face as she sat there speechless, trying to process her mother's words.

"Mrs. Avlon.... Mrs. Avlon. Are you all right?"

Cora stared in a daze at the man before her, unable to process the words coming out of his mouth.

"Are you all right?" he asked again.

Cora looked back at the phone in her hands, not knowing when the call had ended.

"Mrs. Avlon." She heard Mr. Pike say again, his concern for her increasing.

"Um, I..." Looking at her phone again and then back at her lawyer, she spoke, "I have to go."

Without another word, she stood, grabbed her bag, and headed for the door.

Chapter Two

Cora felt the emptiness hit her like a freight train the moment she walked through the front door of her house. The weight of the news pressed down on her so much that she felt as if she could hardly breathe. Without warning, her legs gave out, causing her to crumple to the floor. Uncontrollable sobs wracked her body as she cried for the loss of the man who was her first true love— her father.

She hadn't seen him in person for the past fifteen years and had not spoken more than a few words to him for longer than that. The relationship had soured too much from words spoken in anger and prolonged stubbornness on both their parts. Now she didn't have a chance to tell him how much she regretted everything.

"Daddy..." Cora whimpered.

She drew her knees to her chest as she brought her hands around to cage them in, trying to lessen the tremors she was feeling. She rested her head on her knees, waiting out the slight panic attack.

Why was everything in her life being taken away so

suddenly? First, Joel cheated. Now her father was dead. She doubted she could take on any more life-shattering news. It would destroy her.

When she gathered her energy, she slowly got back on her feet and made her way upstairs. She needed to start packing to go to Oak Harbor, to her childhood home. She needed to be there for her mother. She was sure her sisters would be doing the same thing, and when they finally met up, they would be strong for their mother.

Opening her closet, Cora pulled out her carry-on and began placing the clothes she planned to take with her into it.

Her phone rang. Picking up the device, she realized her daughter was calling.

"Hi, sweetie. I can't talk right now," she answered on the second ring, trying to mask her trembling.

"Mom, what's wrong? I can hear it in your voice," Julia rushed out.

The silence only lasted a few seconds. Cora couldn't hold the gasp that escaped her lips right then and there. "Your grandfather just passed away, sweetie." It came out in less than a whisper.

"Oh my god, Mom. I'm so sorry. I'm on my way. I should be there by this evening. No, scratch that. I'm going to pick Erin up from the airport, and then we'll both be there by nightfall."

A small, sad smile made its way onto Cora's face as she waited for her daughter to finish talking. This trait had always irritated her, and on numerous occasions, she would have to remind Julia to pause and allow others to respond. Today, she was grateful for this one thing she had considered a flaw in her daughter. It took her mind off her somber mood as she marveled at how Julia rattled on without missing a beat.

"Mom... Mom, are you there?"

"Yes, sweetie, I'm here," she responded, not wanting to worry her daughter any more than she knew she was right now.

"I'm just still... in shock, I think. It was just so unexpected." Cora felt the tears stinging her eyes as she tried to blink them away.

"I can't even imagine, Mom, but...just hang in there until we get there, okay?"

"We?" Cora asked, confused.

"Erin, Mom. She's flying down from New York as planned so that we both can be with you, remember?" Julia explained.

"Oh, yes, you did say you were going to pick her up. I didn't know she would have gotten the time off to come—"

"Mom, this is Erin we're talking about," Julia injected. "If you complain of having a cold, her first thought is to book the earliest flight to come and take care of you."

At this, Cora smiled. "That's true," she acquiesced. "Is Brian coming, too, did she say?"

"Um, I don't think so... She didn't mention him coming," Julia revealed.

"Oh, okay." Cora wondered if everything was okay with her daughter and her boyfriend. Ever since that call six months ago, Erin had been deflecting questions about her relationship with Brian. They were still together, that much she was sure of, but it seemed as if their relationship could be coming to an end. Maybe this time together as a family would make her daughter open up to her. Erin had always confided in her mother, so Cora worried when she barely volunteered any news on her relationship.

"Mom, I'm going to head out now... I'm going to drive off soon. I'll call you when I'm at the airport."

"Okay, sweetie, drive safe," Cora cautioned. "Love you."

"Love you too, Mom. Bye."

Placing her cell on the bed, Cora turned back to continue packing for her trip. Then she remembered she had something special in her closet. Pausing, she went back into the closet and brought out the box that contained pictures, souvenirs, and memorabilia from her childhood. That was back when life was simpler—when she and her dad were as tight as the kneaded dough her mother used for her hard dough bread they enjoyed with their hot cocoa.

Cora sat on the edge of her bed and scooted over until she sat in the middle of the huge California King. Opening the box, she removed the items contained inside. There were photos of her as a baby when she received her first bike, lost her first tooth, and received a dollar from the tooth fairy— that was what she had believed until she turned ten.

There were photos with her mom and sisters, but the ones she hovered over were the ones of her father. One of them had him holding her up to put the star on the Christmas tree. Her smile was as bright as the gold trinket she held in her hand, and her father's smile was bright and light just a few inches below her. It was as if they were in their own little world.

A small nostalgic smile graced her lips as her mind transported her to that day. Her father had deemed her tall enough to reach the top of the tree by herself. After explaining to him that she needed to grow a gazillionth time more, her father had whisked her up in his arms, telling her that no matter how much she grew, he would always be there to lift her up to put the star on the tree. She wished she could physically go back to that time just to reclaim the happiness she felt there for a short while.

Her eyes spotted another photo that always gave her joy and a sense of triumph. It was because she knew her father was proud of her. It was the day they had caught the seven-pound brown trout in the lake at Deception Pass. Cora looked down at the skinny preteen, who at that time weighed less than one hundred pounds. Her bright blue-gray eyes stared happily back at her, and a grin split her entire face as she stood beside her equally smiling father. They proudly displayed their catch for the photo to be taken. Cora remembered the feeling of accomplishment and how proud her father had been of her. He had bragged that she was the best at everything she did. Cora reached her hand out, using her finger to trace the outline of her father.

She hadn't realized she was crying until the first drop splashed onto the glossy picture. She quickly reached up to wipe away the tears with the back of her palms.

She was going to miss her father so much. If she could turn back the hands of time, there was so much she would want to do to share with him. Cora replaced the items in the box and slid the lid back on.

Sliding off the bed, she dabbed at her eyes to remove the remaining traces of her tears. She needed to call her sisters to figure out their plans concerning getting down to Oak Harbor for the service. She sighed at the realization she'd not spoken to either of her sisters since her brother-in-law's funeral over a year ago. It was only brief, and then it was five years prior to that. They just weren't that close— at least not anymore. But she had so many stories that made her childhood memorable.

Cora dialed Josephine first. Her hand shook as the phone rang three times before it was answered.

"Hello?" She heard her sister's voice ring through the phone.

"Hey, Josephine," Cora greeted her sister softly.

"Cora." She heard her sister say with relief. "I'm so glad you called," she revealed. "I'm sitting here trying to wrap my mind around this. I don't know; it just seems so surreal."

"I know what you mean," Cora replied. "I'm driving down tomorrow afternoon, and I wanted to know if you and Andrea would want us to meet up and travel down together."

"Cora, that sounds like a wonderful idea, but I won't be able to leave that soon. I'm just going to meet you guys down there the day afterward," Josephine apologized.

"Okay. Have you spoken to Andrea?"

"No...I haven't," Josephine replied. "I've been so busy putting things in place at work and packing. I planned to call her later, though."

"Okay," Cora replied.

The two stayed on the line, neither saying a word to break the silence that ensued after talking about Andrea.

"So I'll see you on Tuesday then," Cora finally strained to say.

"Yes, Tuesday," her sister confirmed.

"Bye, Jo."

"Bye, Cora."

After the two hung up, Cora called her other sister, Andrea.

"Hi, Andrea," Cora greeted as soon as her sister said hello.

Andrea immediately burst into tears at the sound of her sister's voice.

Cora felt her sister's pain tug at her heartstrings, and she broke down in tears, matching the ones coming from the other side of the line.

"Cora..." Andrea cried in anguish. "I...I ca— I can't believe he's gone," she sobbed.

"I know." Cora sniffled as she tried to hold back her tears.

"I called Mom, and she sounded so distraught, so broken. I wish I could have been there to comfort her, you know?"

"I know, sweetie," Cora agreed with her little sister. "I wish I was there too. She needs us, Andrea."

"Yes, I know. I can't even come down until the day afterward. I have an event I'm preparing for."

"That's okay. The girls are coming home to drive down with me in the morning."

"That's good," Andrea expressed. "I haven't seen your girls in a while now. How are they doing?"

"They're good," Cora said, wiping her nose with a tissue.

"Erin is completing her MBA, and Julia is in her final year at Washington State."

"That's great. I'm happy for your girls, Cora," Andrea said.

"How is Aurora?" Cora enquired about Andrea's daughter.

"Oh, Rory is great. She got engaged two months ago."

"Oh, Andrea, that's wonderful news," Cora spoke sincerely.

"Yes, it is. They're planning their wedding for next spring."

"That's so wonderful. I'm happy for her." And she was. She wasn't sure she would get an invite to the wedding, but she was truly happy for her niece.

"So I'll see you Tuesday then."

"Yes."

"Bye."

After hanging up with her sister, Cora went back to packing her luggage, and then she went downstairs to prepare chicken lasagna so that the girls could enjoy it when they finally arrived. She knew it would be a long night, and then they would be on the road in the morning, driving back to Cora's past.

Chapter Three

"Mom, are you sure you have everything you'll need?"

"Yes, sweetie. I'm sure."

The girls had been fussing over their mother the whole morning since they woke and started preparing for their drive to Oak Harbor.

Julia made a breakfast of omelet and toast with orange marmalade and orange juice. Erin made a run to their favorite coffee shop, which was on the next street over. She picked up lattes for her and Julia and an espresso macchiato for Cora.

Cora loved the rich flavor and the aroma of her coffee. She took a sip, enjoying the crisp taste it left on her tongue. The dollop of foamy milk went well with the spicy, woody flavor and gave the perfect kick-start to her day. This was always her go-to beverage, especially when the day-to-day bustle of life became too much to handle.

After breakfast, the three ladies piled into Cora's olive-green Land Rover and took off for Oak Harbor. Erin opted to drive even though Oak Harbor was less than two hours away from Cora's home in West Bellevue, Seattle. She hadn't been back in over fifteen years, which spoke to how deep the rift of resentment had been between her and her father. She still couldn't believe he was gone.

Erin pulled onto I-5, starting the hour and a half journey to Cora's childhood home.

"Mom," Julia started.

"Yeah, Jules?"

"You know I was thinking... we don't know anything about your heritage, Erin and me, that is. We've only been to Oak Harbor once, and even then, we were too young to remember much. How come you've never really spoken about your hometown?"

The question threw Cora. It was true she hadn't spoken much about growing up in Oak Harbor. She had many good memories growing up there, but some bad ones had pretty much overshadowed the good ones.

"I'm sorry, Mom, you don't have to say anything. I didn't mean to upset you," Julia quickly assured at her mother's lack of response. Cora hadn't seen the warning look and subtle head shake Erin had given her sister in the rearview.

"Jules, I'm not upset," Cora refuted softly. "It's just... your question caught me off guard. It made me think about some of the mistakes I made raising you girls. You don't know your family heritage because I turned my back on it and kept you away. And honestly, that was selfish of me. I should never have done that." Cora took in a jagged breath.

Cora had been so angry with her father that it affected all the relationships in her life— even that of her daughters. At the time, though, she thought if she didn't speak about her family, it would make the estrangement easier to cope with.

The few times her mother had visited her and the girls, she

had made it abundantly clear that she didn't want to talk about her father and, subsequently, anything that had to do with him, including Oak Harbor.

"Mom, we're fine. We're not upset with you. You were and still are a great mom," Erin weighed in. "Besides, we had Grandma Annie and Grandpa Joe. We didn't feel cheated."

Cora turned to smile at her daughter. "I know you're trying to make me feel better, sweetie, but it doesn't excuse my actions."

From the back seat, Julia reached her hand over the front to rest it on her mother's right shoulder in comfort. Cora stretched her right hand over to rest it on the hand on her shoulder.

"I love you girls so much," she stressed, squeezing Julia's hand. "I really do want you to know about me, who I was before I met your father and left Oak Harbor."

"Mom—"

"I want you to know."

Erin looked worriedly over at her mother but kept silent. Julia didn't say anything, but her hand remained on her mother's shoulder as she scooted forward and rested her head on the back of her seat.

Cora sifted through the memories that were fresh enough for her to share. "Growing up in Oak Harbor was a wonderful experience," she answered truthfully.

"Your aunts and I, we had so much fun growing up there. We were so close— like three peas in a pod." They were all born two years apart but still did everything together.

She smiled as she remembered the name they had been given by their friends back in middle school, Triple H.

"We went to the beach every chance we got, hiked the many trails found on the island, and Dad took us with him on his fishing trips occasionally."

"That explains why you love the outdoors so much," Julia mused.

"And the water," Erin chimed in.

"Yes, it is." Cora smiled.

"We had the privilege to enjoy the things that tourists come to the island to do, like zip-lining, kayaking, whale watching, and bird watching. We did it all." Cora listed the activities she could remember, but they had enjoyed so many other things.

"Dad was an outdoors person, and he wanted us to enjoy the amazingness of our island." All these memories were opening up so many emotions within her. She was happy that she got to enjoy these activities, but she was also sad that, in the end, it seemed as if their father had been grooming them to be excellent hosts who could provide their guests with expert advice on the island and its attractions.

"Dad wanted us to stay and go to college on the island. That way, we could learn the business and take it over when he chose to retire or—" Cora hesitated to finish her sentence but slowly started again. "When I chose to go out of state for college, he was furious. I tried to get him to understand that running the inn wasn't my dream. I wanted more than that, but he wouldn't listen or accept that, and we barely spoke in my final months of high school. The day before I was to leave for Berkley, we had a huge blow-up..." Cora took in a well-needed gulp of air before releasing it as her mind went back to that day.

"What about what I want, Dad?" Cora asked, throwing her hands in the air as she gave her father a pointed look. She wouldn't back down this time.

Her father looked at her, the anger radiating off him as his eyes narrowed until all she could see were the misty blue of his eyes.

Cora stepped back in shock. She had never seen him this angry before.

He raised his hand, and she took another tentative step back. He pointed his index finger at her.

"If you leave—"

27

Cora shook herself out of the memory. It was such a painful one that had prompted the end of her relationship with her father— the first man she ever fell in love with, the man she once looked up to and loved with all her heart.

How could he not want her to have her own life— chart her own course? Since the age of nine, she had wanted to be a journalist. She told him on numerous occasions.

"There is plenty to report on here. Why would you want to go anywhere else?"

On those occasions, she would just smile and agree with him. Maybe if she hadn't been so compliant, perhaps if she had been more adamant about what she wanted to do, he would have taken her seriously. It wouldn't have gotten to the point it did. That had always been her problem. She hadn't wanted to disappoint her father.

"Mom?"

Cora looked over at the driver's seat to see Erin glancing between her and the road with concern etched on her face.

"You had that faraway look," she explained.

"Oh, I'm sorry, sweetie. I'm doing that a lot aren't I?"

Erin gave her a sympathetic smile, and she felt Julia give her shoulder a slight squeeze.

"It's just so hard to know that we didn't get to have a relationship because of his anger and stubbornness." She sighed sadly.

"He didn't get to see you guys grow up and become the wonderful women you are today. I'm more sad that you didn't get to have a genuine relationship with my mom, with your aunts and cousins." She shook her head as her eyes glazed over with her tears. "So many wasted years." She exhaled.

Cora felt so much regret. Her rift with her father should not have prevented her from seeing her mother. If she were honest with herself, then she would have realized that it had hurt her just as much that her mother had said nothing while she stood by as her father had when he cut into her with his words. These actions to Cora meant that she would always stand by him even when he was wrong and at the expense of a relationship with her children and grandchildren.

That was all under the bridge now. She needed to mend the relationship with her mother. Time was short, and life was unpredictable.

Erin exited I-5 at Exit 226 and turned left onto the state highway. Soon, they would be on the Deception Pass Bridge and close to Oak Harbor.

Cora looked out the window as she thought about all the events that had occurred in her life in the past six months: She won an award for investigative journalism, she found out her husband cheated on her with their housekeeper, kicked him out of their home, filed for a divorce, her father died, and now here she was on the highway heading in the direction of a town she hadn't set foot in for over fifteen years. Life seemed so arbitrary.

She didn't know what to expect going back to Oak Harbor, and she had to admit that she was anxious. Fifteen years was a long time to be away from a place. A lot could change in that period. A lot could change in less time than that.

"Did I ever tell you about the time your aunt and I got busted for going to a concert in Seattle?"

"No way!" The sisters gaped at her.

Cora turned to them with a mischievous glint in her eyes.

"I have gotten into my fair share of trouble," Cora revealed, a short laugh escaping her lips. "I wasn't a wild child, but I did have my moments of acting out."

Erin grinned at the statement. "Our mom, the rebel," Julia marveled behind her.

"Andrea and I were in high school at the time. We asked Mom and Dad if we could go with some friends, but they refused."

"So what did you do? How did you guys make it to the concert?" Julia asked, impatient to wait for her mother to finish.

"We didn't make it to the concert." Cora laughed at this, her mind going back to the disastrous trip.

"You guys ready to go?" Brent asked. He and Cora had been dating at the time, and he was the designated driver.

"Yeah, Brent, just give me a minute," she told him.

Cora turned to Andrea. She noticed Andrea was biting her thumb as she rocked from side to side, signifying that she was having second thoughts.

"Cora, I don't think we should do this. What if Mom calls Hailey's mom and finds out we aren't actually at her house, or we end up in a high-speed chase and the police post our photos on Prime Time?"

Cora raised an eyebrow as she considered the latter part of her sister's concerns and her imagination.

"A, there is no way we would end up in a high speed chase, you're projecting." She placed her hands on her sister's shoulders and looked her in the eyes. "We won't get caught," she assured Andrea.

"And if we do, I'll take the fall since it was my idea anyway. Plus, I'm older."

Andrea gave her a tight-lipped smile that was more of a grimace before turning to the waiting car where Brent, Hailey, and two more of Cora's classmates waited.

Pulling away from Hailey's house, the group made their way to Seattle. Only, they didn't make it to the concert.

"What happened, Mom?" Erin looked over at her, struggling to stay focused on the road while listening to her mother.

"We got pulled over a few miles away from the concert for a busted taillight, and would you believe that my date forgot his license?" Cora couldn't contain her smile. "Andrea had predicted a car chase, but we got busted for a taillight and driving without a license." Cora finally burst out in hysterics. It wasn't comical then, but it was now.

Her daughters joined in the laughter, happy the mood lifted even for a short while.

Chapter Four

Cora looked up as Deception Pass Bridge came into view. It connected Seattle to the fourth largest island in the contiguous United States, Whidbey Island, of which Oak Harbor was one of its largest cities. It was the same magnificent edifice since Cora lived in Oak Harbor.

The bridge arched so regally over the silent flowing passage of water below. From above, the blue-green waters looked serene but ran very deep, and if you didn't know what you were doing, the violent currents below the surface could sweep you out to sea. Still, it was a wonderful sight to behold, especially during the sunsets, where the bold orange hue of the sun was as prominent as the flames of a wildfire burning at night. Its descent caused the waters to come to life as the slight ripples on the surface shimmered brightly. When it dropped below the bridge to touch the water, the transition of the sky and water from blue to orange and then to a pinkish hue was something out of a glossy-paged nature magazine.

Cora felt her chest tighten the farther along the bridge they drove. They were almost at their destination, and she was anxious. She wondered if everything was the way she had left it. She worried about the kind of emotions seeing the town again after fifteen years would evoke.

The sign appeared in the distance. She knew what was on it before they made it close enough to read the black letterings. It was arched over the elliptical board sign that read **Welcome to Whidbey Island** across a light-blue background displaying the popular water activities the island was famous for, with two eagles on pedestals with beavers below them on either side.

Finally, they pulled past Oak Harbor's welcome sign. The town was home to the Garry Oak trees, the Whidbey Island Naval Air Station, many parks, water bodies, and landforms that captured the vibrancy of nature.

Cora felt like a tourist marveling at the beautiful Cascade Mountains on the horizon; the craggy snowcapped tops were a stark contrast to the clear blue skies making the whole range look so ethereal. If she was desperate for a reminder of how Hallmark-worthy her hometown could be, she only had to look west to see a glimpse of Mt. Rainier. Its looming dark presence from across the coast was overshadowed by the blue skies, appearing as an apparition. It had been too long.

At first, she thought nothing much had changed, only to realize so much had changed. The familiar buildings she grew up seeing were still around. The Whidbey Playhouse on Midway Blvd was still operational. As far as she could tell, it was very well maintained. She could also recognize a few of the local small diners and eateries that she used to frequent when she went on dates back in high school. There was Oak Terrace, famous for its late brunches and seafood specials. Capt. O'Malley was widely popular for their strawberry cheesecake desserts and coffee ice cream fudge, which was a family special. Cora wondered if Jenny, one of her friends from high school, had stayed to run the family business or if, like her, she had chosen to get away from this town.

"This place is like a dream," Julia said.

"You can say that again," Erin agreed.

"That's why tourists visit all year round. There is so much for them to do here, and the pictures they take are just beautiful."

Her girls were entranced.

"There are a few gardens and vineyards that I would like us to go to after the funeral if you guys are up to it." Her offer was immediately accepted, and she smiled at how much her girls already loved the quaint little town where their mother had grown up in.

As they drove past downtown Oak Harbor, she could see this part of town had the most development. They drove past a few new malls, fashion stores, a movie theater, a commercial business building, and a parking garage. This had become the business district of the town.

Cora's heartbeat rapidly intensified when they turned onto 8th Avenue, also known as the Avenue of the Oaks. They were now only about five miles from the family house and the inn. Both sides of the road were lined with the famous Garry Oak trees from which the town's name was penned. They were magnificent in their expanse. They stood tall on either side like a guard, not much foliage with their wide branches and small, spacey pinnate leaves.

Cora clasped and unclasped her hands in her lap, a nervous tic of hers as they left Regatta Drive onto Maui Avenue. Soon they were on Torpedo Road and only five minutes away from the turn to the property.

"Turn here, sweetie," Cora instructed her daughter at the same time the GPS chimed in. A minute afterward, they were driving past the sign that read Welcome to Willberry Inn, Restaurant and Property.

The property was a total of ten acres and sat overlooking Crescent Harbor. It consisted of the family house, the inn, a barn that was remodeled into a restaurant that Cora had never seen, along with countless fruit trees and several oak trees that the area was so famous for.

The long semi-arched driveway was hedged in by well-maintained boxwood and fire and ice daylilies. Cora admired the pleasant contrast between the lush green shrubbery and the purple irises popping out between the rows. She took the time to admire and reacquaint herself with the inn's exterior on the two-minute drive up to the house.

The inn was a three-story old-world colonial home with a few modernized features. Wider, sliding windows replaced the narrow ones that were once featured. It had balconies surrounding the other two floors so that each guest could sit out on the deck to enjoy the scenic views that perpetuated the entire property, namely that of the tranquil harbor from the upper floors. A wall of vibrant aromatic flowers lined the walkway leading up to the entrance.

Cora wondered if the guests could still appreciate the cozy antiquated rooms that had been a part of its appeal since before she was born.

As soon as the car stopped and they got out, the front door of the family house opened, and her mother walked out.

"Cora?"

Her mother sounded surprised.

"Hi, Mom."

Cora walked to meet her mother as she stepped down the three short steps that led from the front porch. Her mother stood before her looking frail and tired. Her once lustrous chestnut brown hair was now peppered with gray and looked a lot thinner than she'd ever seen it. Her brown eyes were rimmed red and held so much sadness.

"Mom, I'm so sorry," Cora started to say before she was pulled into her mother's tight embrace.

"I'm so happy you're here. I wish it were under better circumstances, but you're here now." Her mother breathed against her cheek.

Cora felt her tears begin to run as something in her gave way. A guttural sound escaped her lips, and her heart clenched and unclenched within her chest as she released the heavy pressure that had built up there.

Becky Hamilton held on to her daughter tightly, allowing her to release the grief, the regrets, the anger, and the frustration she had been holding in. Cora knew her mother understood how she felt. Even though Cora hadn't spoken to her father in so many years, Becky knew that she still loved him very much, and it was Samuel's stubbornness that had gotten in the way of them reconciling.

Becky looked over her shoulder to see Cora's daughters standing there, looking at their interaction with sadness in their eyes.

"Erin, Julia. It's so good to see you. What has it been? Four years since the last time I visited?"

"I think it was longer than that, Grandma." Erin gave her grandmother a feeble smile.

At the sound of their interaction, Cora straightened up, stepping out of her mother's embrace.

"Well, don't just stand there... come give your dear old grandma a hug."

Erin and Julia walked up to their grandmother and took turns giving her a light hug.

"I'm sorry about Granddad, Grandma."

Becky gave Julia a sad smile, her eyes glistening with tears. Cora reached for her mother's hand and squeezed.

"You'll get through this, Mom," she promised. "I'm here

now, and Andrea and Josephine will be here by tomorrow. We'll get everything sorted."

The front door opened, and a man who resembled her father in looks and stature stepped through it. Cora's heart skipped a beat. She turned her head to collect her thoughts and calm her breathing before turning back to the man making his way toward them.

"Cora." He reached out for her. "I'm so glad you're here," he spoke sincerely, the gruffness in his deep voice trying to hide the sadness.

"Hi, Uncle Luke," she replied as she went over to hug him. He completely towered over her five-foot-five frame at six-feet-two, so she was completely enveloped in his arms by the hug.

Cora wanted to stay in his arms. It reminded her so much of the times her father used to hug her; those times she used to feel so sheltered, so loved. Uncle Luke even smelled like him. Reluctantly, she pulled away from her uncle and plastered a smile on her tear-stained face.

"Thanks for being here, Uncle Luke...for Mom, I mean."

"Cora," her uncle started in a serious tone, "I love you guys very much, and Sam was my brother. I had to be here."

Cora was grateful for Uncle Luke. He was such an honorable man. She hadn't spoken to him in a couple of years, but she knew he was one person she and her sisters could depend on if they ever needed him.

"Are these your girls?" he asked, looking over her shoulder.

Cora turned to them. "Yes. Uncle, this is Erin and Julia." She gestured.

"Hi, Uncle Luke," Erin spoke meekly, holding out her hand for a handshake.

Uncle Luke looked at the hand before him and looked back at Erin.

"Dear, we don't do that here. We're family. Besides, you're

the daughter of my favorite niece," he stated. "A proper hug is in order."

Erin dropped her hand and smiled apologetically.

Uncle Luke held his outstretched hands before her, and Erin walked into the embrace. After releasing her, he turned to Julia and repeated the gesture. Cora's heart warmed over at the display of familial affection.

"Your aunt Stacy and Maria are inside," Becky told her daughter.

With that, the group made their way inside to greet the rest of the family, who was already there.

"So, Cora, where are your sisters?" That question came from her aunt Stacy, who was trying to settle herself comfortably on the couch, her motorized walker not too far from her reach.

"Oh, they will arrive tomorrow," she explained.

"That's great. I haven't seen them in a while. I'm sad that a tragedy brings us all back together but happy that we will all be under one roof again." Her aunt spoke with hope intermingled with sadness.

"I'm glad too," Cora agreed, although she felt some apprehension.

After Cora and the girls freshened up, they got their luggage. Cora had opted to stay in her old room, but the girls chose to take rooms at the inn. After placing her luggage at the foot of the stairs, she followed the girls and her mother over to the inn. It was a five-minute walk from the house, so she used the time to point out memorable places along the path to her girls.

The opulent winding double staircase in the middle of the foyer was the first thing the girls noticed, and their appreciation of this filled Cora with pride.

To the left of the front door stood the reception area and a woman who seemed to be around her age or maybe a little younger. She had raven-colored hair and big doe-shaped eyes behind a pair of round spectacles and a bright smile on her face. She wore a baby-blue tunic top with the words Willberry Inn stitched over the right pocket. She was beautiful.

"Cora, girls, let me introduce you to the heart of this place," her mother said, steering them over to the desk.

"This is Marg Lewis."

Chapter Five

"*If you leave, don't even think about coming back here. You won't be welcomed.*"

"*How... how can you say that? I'm your daughter.*"

"*If you leave, you're no daughter of mine.*"

Cora woke with a start. Her head pounded, and her heart beat rapidly, threatening to break through her rib cage. That was the most intense dream she'd had about her father in a very long time. She looked around the dark room, trying to remember where she was. This wasn't her bedroom back in Seattle— that much she was sure of.

She shook her head to clear the fog and swung her feet over the edge of the bed. It all came back to her suddenly. She was in her old bedroom back home. She was here to attend her father's funeral.

Reaching over, she switched on the bed lamp, lightly illuminating her room in its dim glow. The old alarm clock read 4:45 a.m. Her sisters would be arriving this morning, but that was still a few hours away, and she doubted anyone in the house had even stirred in their beds. Still, she couldn't go back to sleep. Rising, she turned on the overhead light, bathing the room in its brightness.

She had been surprised that her room had looked the same since the last time she was there, but she hadn't gotten the chance to inspect it thoroughly. After giving the girls a tour of the inn and getting them settled, then catching up with her uncle Luke, his wife, and her aunt, she had fallen asleep as soon as her head hit the pillow.

Now in the quietness of the morning, she thought it convenient to look over her room— to relive old memories.

When she first stepped into the room, she was surprised to see her double bed made with her floral duvet and all her pillows and cushions neatly stacked along the headboard. Even her favorite brown bear was propped up against them.

Cora walked over to her closet to see all her old clothes were still hung up. Her toiletries were still displayed on her dresser, and the fluffy pink area rug was still at the foot of her bed.

She walked over to the wall shelves by her window, where her trophies were still on display. Reaching over, she ran her hand over her track medals from elementary school. She was surprised at how shiny they still were as if they were polished regularly. The trophies and medals from her softball and volleyball tournaments in high school were front and center. She had been a great athlete. She and her father had always bonded over that and her avid love for the outdoors like him.

Cora reached over to pick up the last award she had won as a member of Oak Harbor High's volleyball team. She had been voted MVP for her performance the entire season and had won herself an athletic scholarship to Berkeley.

Cora smiled sadly; that had been a bittersweet moment for her. Her dream had finally started to take shape, which meant her father's anger and disagreement with her decision had come full circle.

Silent tears slid down her cheeks as she imagined how different that moment could have been if only her father had put aside his unrealistic expectations and supported her the way she had wanted him to.

"Cora... are you awake?"

The knock on the door and her mother's voice dragged her out of her pensive thoughts.

"Morning, Mom. You can come in." As her mother stepped into the room, Cora averted her eyes, not wanting her to see the wetness on her face.

Her mother hadn't spoken since she came into the room a minute ago, which caused Cora to turn her head to look at her.

"You know he was so proud of you that day." Becky gestured with her pointer finger at the object Cora held.

Cora looked down at the trophy, surprised by her mother's revelation. *Her father was proud of her?* That day he had blown his top after she had confirmed that she would be taking the scholarship to Berkeley.

She put the trophy back before turning to her mother with a forlorn look.

"Mom, that's not how I remember it," she stated, looking despondent. "The words he spoke—" Cora shuddered at the memory fresh from her dream. "To this day, I still can't wrap my mind around it; the anger, the disappointment for achieving something so great and being rewarded for it."

"Cora, I—"

"I just want to know what I did that was so wrong for him to cut me off like I no longer meant anything to him. Like I was no longer welcomed in this family. And you..." Cora sucked in a sharp breath before turning away from her mother, not knowing how to finish her statement or if it was even wise to do so now.

A pregnant pause filled the room as her mother struggled to find the right words. After some time, she finally spoke.

"I know you might not be able to accept this now, Cora, but Sam loved you, and he regretted the way things went. He—"

Cora harrumphed as she whirled to face her mother again.

"Mom, I know he's your husband, but how can you stand there and tell me he regretted what he said— what he did?" she asked in disbelief.

Her mother gulped as she looked at Cora with regret in her light-brown eyes.

Cora looked away from her as she tried to control her emotions. "It doesn't matter now. He's gone."

"Cora—"

"I don't want to talk about it now, Mom."

Becky opened and closed her mouth, finding it difficult to speak.

Cora felt so many emotions. She was mourning her father's death, but still, she harbored so much unresolved resentment toward him because of the way he had hurt her so deeply. Her mother's defense of his treatment of her had triggered her frustration. She tried to control the words that left her mouth, but she knew the ones she left unspoken, and her tone had rattled her mother. She hadn't meant to upset her, not at this time when the pain of losing her husband was so raw.

Now she could throw her feeling of regret into the mix of emotions.

"Okay, I'm going to my room. The restaurant will cater breakfast for the family. We'll be having it out by the patio around seven o'clock." She heard her mother say.

"Okay, I'm gonna go for a run, but I should be back before then," Cora informed her.

Cora watched her mother open the door, but she didn't step through it. Instead, she turned back, her eyes filled with sadness even as she gave her a small smile.

"I'll see you when you get back." She pulled the door shut as she left. Cora allowed the tears to fall freely once more.

* * *

The cold morning air stung Cora's lungs, her breath coming out as short puffs of vapor. She willed her burning calves to keep moving forward, maintaining the pace she had set for herself. Her mind raced ahead of her feet.

How could her mother expect her to believe the words she had spoken? She was there when Sam had ripped into her. She saw how depressed Cora had been after the confrontation. Yet she stood in Cora's bedroom today, telling her that he had regretted his actions. There was no way Cora could accept that — not unless Samuel Arthur Hamilton rose from the dead to tell her so himself.

She also felt the guilt creep up again as she recalled how she had spoken to her mother. Her mother needed time to mourn without adding the weight of the accusation of her complicity in Cora being ostracized from her family back then.

At times like these, her thoughts also wandered to her soon-to-be ex-husband. She thought about Joel and what he could be doing back in Seattle— probably playing house with their one-time housekeeper. She had heard from a few of their mutual friends that he was seen at a few establishments with her and had even heard that he was planning on marrying her and moving to Florida as soon as the divorce was finalized. The news had devastated Cora even though she did her best to hide it from the others, especially her girls.

Still, she couldn't help the loneliness she felt now and wished they were still together. At least she could've burdened him with her problems. He would have cuddled with her as she unloaded, then he would gently run his fingers through her hair as he helped her calm her inner turmoil.

She only had herself to depend on to get through all this, including his betrayal.

She had decided to go for a run for this reason—to clear her mind and the tension from her body. So far, her body had begun to relax a mile into her intended six-mile run toward Smith Park over on 9th Avenue, but her mind was taking its time to cooperate.

Feeling the need to kick-start the endorphins secretion, she took time to admire the huge populous oak trees scattered throughout the vicinity. They were the most notable attraction on this side of the island because of their numbers. Their mushroom-shaped tops and the contorted branches reached out in every way like the fingers of old evil witches you read about in scary tales. The silver-gray barks were distinct from all the other deciduous trees found on that side of the continental US. It was an amazing sight to behold.

As she made her way to the park, her heart rate had evened out considerably, and her breathing was less labored. More importantly, her mind had taken on a state of peacefulness, blocking out the troublesome thoughts that continuously plagued her.

Cora arrived at the park entrance, a national treasure in its own right consisting of nearly only Garry Oak trees, some being over three hundred years old. She made a beeline south of the park and stopped before the iridescent waters of Puget Sound and the snowcapped Olympic mountains that formed the most beautiful backdrop over the ocean.

This had always been one of her favorite places back when she lived here— this and Crescent Harbor, which was in her backyard. This was the perfect spot to watch the magnificently gracious orcas' dorsal fins split the water's surface, the dark rubbery back making its appearance afterward. It was even more stunning to watch them leap in the air before diving under the surface. No picture could accurately capture the tangible experience of such displays.

Even though the circumstances were tragic, she was happy to be here.

Cora spent about fifteen minutes admiring the view before her. She needed to head back soon if she wanted to make it in time for breakfast.

She made it back with fifteen minutes to spare. As the house came into view, she noticed two new cars parked beside hers under the open carport to the side. *Had her sisters arrived already?*

Cora could hear voices coming from the family room as soon as she stepped through the front door. She made her way in that direction. Everyone was turned away from her, but she quickly recognized her sisters based on specific features. Standing at five feet six, Andrea was taller than Josephine by about two inches, and her brown hair was much lighter than Josephine's sandy-colored hair with streaks of blond. They both still looked in shape. They hadn't changed that much since she last saw them over a year ago at the funeral.

As if sensing her presence, her sisters, along with the others, turned to face her. Andrea's light blue eyes showed relief, while Josephine's dark brown ones looked cautious.

"Cora," Andrea breathed out with a sad smile as she made her way to her sister.

Cora opened her arms for the hug that was coming. Andrea clung to her fervently, making her heart swell and break at the same time at the vulnerability. Cora looked back at Josephine, who remained rooted to her spot with a small smile that didn't quite reach her eyes.

Chapter Six

"Hi, Cora," Josephine greeted as she folded her arms around her body, hugging herself.

"Hey, Jo." Cora gave her sister a friendly smile, noting the difference in her greeting. She and Andrea had grown apart over the years and still had a ways to go in repairing their bond, but she perceived the greater hurdle would be her relationship with her baby sister, Jo.

"I'm happy to see you," she expressed genuinely. "Both of you." She turned to Andrea, smiling happily. And she was.

"It's good to be home," Josephine expressed as she looked away from them.

Cora felt a stab of guilt at her statement as she deliberately chose not to acknowledge Cora's happiness at their presence. She wished that there wasn't such a wide chasm between them, that she could reach over and hug her and tell her that it would all be okay. She knew she was hurting as much as the others, even if her expressions weren't as reflective of this.

Cora glanced around the room, noting the apprehension on

her mother's face and the looks of curiosity from her aunt, uncle, and her nieces.

"The girls should be coming over in the next few minutes. Breakfast will be served shortly," her mother announced, breaking the awkward silence that had enveloped the room.

Cora was happy about the distraction. "Okay, Mom," she acknowledged.

"Tracey, Aurora, I'm so happy to see you," she said, smiling at her two nieces.

"It has been a minute, Aunt Cora." Tracey came over to give her aunt a quick hug. Rory did the same.

"I'm happy to be here, too, Aunt Cora." Rory's light-brown eyes were so reflective of her mother's crinkled at the corners from the genuineness of her statement. Cora reached out and lightly touched her ginger-colored hair.

She had always marveled at her niece's hair because no one in the family had that hair color. It was such a unique hue that Cora could only assume she had inherited from her father— a father whose name none of them knew.

She and her sisters had all, for the most part, inherited their mother's chestnut-brown hair. Cora's girls also had light-brown hair, and Tracy inherited her mother's sandy-brown hair. Rory had been the exception.

"I'm going to go freshen up. I'll be back shortly," she informed everyone before heading for her room.

When Cora finally made it downstairs, she walked to the back door and out onto the back porch. She spotted her family already seated around the long oak table on the patio.

The patio, which was an extension of their back wrap-around veranda, was a sizeable semi-enclosed area with a high open ceiling that could be covered in the event of rainfall or excess sunlight by the retractable pergola sliding roof. The floor's montage of varying cuts of flagstones resembled leaves of a deciduous tree going through the four seasons. They were accentuated by the bamboo chairs with vivid red, green, and orange cushions and pillows, giving the area a warm, lively aura.

The space was also equipped with a charcoal barrel grill and smoker in one corner and a firepit in the center, indicating its purpose for family get-togethers and barbecues.

Descending the three short steps from the porch, she walked over to her family.

Erin was the first to notice her. "Hey, Mom."

"Hi, sweetie," she greeted back. "Did you sleep well?"

"Yes, I really like my room. It was... homey. Jules was being a baby, though, so she slept in my room." At Erin's revelation, Julia stuck her tongue out at her sister like a little child, making Cora and the others at the table chuckle at the display.

She was happy to see that the mood had shifted to a lighter one since she left.

"Come sit by me." Erin patted the empty chair beside her.

Cora noticed that the only other two available seats were beside Josephine and her mother. She gladly walked over and sat beside her daughter, thinking it was the safer choice.

Cora's mouth salivated at the decadent assortment of foods spread out on the table. As if on cue, she heard the slight rumble of her stomach. She hadn't realized she was so hungry, but then again, she hadn't eaten much the day before. After their mother said grace, Cora helped herself to a reasonable portion of scrambled eggs, bacon, sausage, toast, and fruit as the conversation resumed.

"So, Erin, your mother told me that you're finishing up your MBA in advertising?" Andrea asked as she dug into her plate of scrambled eggs.

Cora looked up at her daughter, who was beaming with pride.

"Yes, I have two more exams, and then I'm completing my internship," she explained. "The agency I'm working with is considering me for the junior marketing manager position after I'm done." Her smile grew wider at this, while her green eyes were bright with hope.

"Wow, that's wonderful!" Andrea exclaimed. "I'm so happy for you, Erin. That truly is amazing news. You should be so proud of yourself, honey."

"Thanks, Aunt Andrea."

Cora smiled at the interaction, happy that her strained relationship with her sisters hadn't hindered their interest in her children. The conversations continued to center on the younger versions of themselves, and she was grateful for that as it gave her better insights into her nieces' lives.

"James couldn't make it because he has an important court case to argue. I didn't want him to be distracted because this is a huge case that could make or break his career." Aurora explained why her fiancé hadn't made the trip to Oak Harbor with her.

Cora could see how much Aurora cared for the man who had captured her heart by her giddy smiles and her constant soft touches of the huge princess-cut diamond that rested on her left ring finger. Young love was always so innocent and passionate in its expressions. She was happy that her niece had found someone she wanted to spend the rest of her life with, and she prayed it would last.

"I'm telling you, your father swallowed those bird peppers like a champ. His face was so red. You could see the steam coming out of his ears as he sweated bullets. Then he said he couldn't breathe. I panicked and called Mama. After the three glasses of milk and water, Mama called the doctor. He gave him some antihistamine. It knocked him out like a baby." Uncle Luke shook his head in wonder as he recounted the day he had dared their father to eat ten red hot peppers.

"Would you believe when Pa came home and Mama told him what happened, instead of being relieved that Sam was okay, he called us both before him and tanned our hides?" He guffawed, bringing his large, slightly wrinkled hands up to run them through his graying black hair.

Cora laughed along with the others at the comicalness of her father's whole ordeal. She was happy to hear these stories. They were intimate memories of her dad's life before becoming an adult and a father himself. She was grateful for this version of him that she hadn't gotten to meet.

After breakfast, Uncle Luke offered to take the girls sight-seeing around Oak Harbor, to which the four girls eagerly agreed.

Becky offered to give her daughters a full tour of the inn and restaurant, and Aunt Maria went with Aunt Stacy for a stroll as her limited mobility meant she needed someone by her side at all times.

Entering the inn, they walked into the foyer and made their way to the front desk. "This is Marg Lewis, our esteemed receptionist slash assistant manager. She has been here for the past ten years, and she is invaluable to this place," their mother was saying as Marg walked around the reception desk to shake the sisters' hands.

"I'm so happy to meet you all in person. I've heard so much about you," she heard Marg say as she greeted her sisters. Her bright smile was infectious, and Cora noticed that both sisters smiled back at her, probably touched by her warmth.

Cora had decided that she very much liked Marg from the day before, and if she had planned to stay in Oak Harbor, they would probably become fast friends. She noted that as happy as Marg was, there seemed to be some underlying pain that wasn't so easily caught unless you were paying keen attention to her mannerisms. Cora had caught her yesterday with a melancholy look on her face which was quickly replaced when she saw her. Cora had wondered where such a look of sadness could be stemming from in a person with such a bubbly personality.

After they toured the inn, they made their way over to the restaurant.

The restaurant was a remodeled barn house. The room was very spacious, with large front and rear glass windows framed in dark walnut-stained wood that matched the interior of the building. The rustic-looking wooden tables and chairs were evenly spaced throughout the room, leaving much room for maneuvering. The high gambrel roof was decorated with low-hanging lights on the far corners and ceiling fans in the middle of the rafter beams from front to back. The ambiance was one of comfort and intimacy. Cora thought everything looked beautiful and cozy.

"This is Daniel or, as we all call him, Chef Daniel." Her mother gestured to the tall, lean man dressed in his gray chef whites.

"It's a pleasure to meet you all. Your parents spoke highly of you all," the man said, giving a slight bend. Cora noticed he had a slight accent, maybe French.

"This is Rick, our sous chef." Her mother then introduced the man on the right in a black chef jacket. Like Daniel, he was quite tall and wispy. He had short black hair.

"It's a pleasure to meet you," he greeted politely.

Moving on, their mother gestured toward three young girls that couldn't be over twenty-one. "These lovely girls are Suzie, Pat, and Kay." They all greeted Cora and her sisters with a warm smile that she returned.

"They work part-time as waitresses because they're still in college. They go to Colombia," their mother explained.

After the greetings, they made their way back to the house, but Josephine had opted to go for a walk.

Cora felt the urge to follow her.

After making it to the house's front porch, she paused at the steps, feeling conflicted. She knew her sister didn't necessarily want to be around them, more specifically her, but she had to try to reach out to her.

"You guys go on inside without me. I'm going to stay out here a little," she informed the two women on the porch.

"Okay, honey," her mother replied. Andrea turned to look at her with concern, but she didn't say anything.

Cora headed in the direction her sister had gone. She passed the patio and took the paved walkway that led down to the dock by the harbor. She passed the large flower garden and sitting area her father had gifted her mother with all those years ago. She would have stopped to admire its beauty, but she was on a mission.

When she finally made her way down the path to the area that formed the property's border with beautifully trimmed hedges, Cora was met with the beautiful sight of the harbor, Cascade Range, and the ice-capped Mt. Rainier. It featured prominently blue-green waters decorated with a few sailboats and small fishing vessels below. This was her second-best place on the island— her backyard.

Cora headed toward the dock where her father's motorboat was tied and bobbing slightly to and fro as the waves beat against it. But even before she made it, she could see that Josephine wasn't there. She wondered where she could be. She decided to use the walkway that led from the inn to head back. Various seasonal fruit trees lined the path, which her mother used for her delicious jams and preserves.

She found Josephine sitting on the old swing attached to the old oak not too far from the inn.

Steeling herself, she walked up to her sister, whose back was to her.

On impulse, Cora reached out her hands to hold the ropes of the swing pulling it backward before releasing it to swing forward. From the side, she watched as her sister moved back and forth for a few seconds before she spoke.

"Hey."

"Hey," Josephine returned without looking toward her.

"Are you angry with me, Jo?" Cora finally asked after a full minute had passed.

Josephine abruptly stopped the swing. She exhaled before looking up at Cora.

Cora felt a punch to her gut at the sadness in her sister's red, puffy eyes.

"I honestly don't think now is the time," Jo replied, looking out at the water.

Cora's heart panged in her chest, and she knew it would take more than a couple of hours or a few days for her and her sisters to mend their pain. She just had to have some patience.

Before Cora turned on her heel to walk back to the house, she whispered, "All right then. Just know I love you, Jo."

Chapter Seven

"Samuel Arthur Hamilton, a loving and devoted husband, father, grandfather, brother, uncle... No words can adequately express the loss that we, his family, are feeling, but we are thankful for the time we got to spend with him here on earth and for all the wonderful memories that we now hold close to our hearts."

Cora squeezed her mother's hand in comfort as she sat through the service with a look of despair. The tears steadily made their way down her mother's cheeks and dripped onto Cora's hand, clasping hers.

Cora frantically wiped her tears as the realness of the moment took hold of her. Her family sat in the front pews of the church, all dressed in black. Non-family members filled the pews behind them as a show of support.

Andrea, who was on the other side of their mother, held her waist, keeping her upright and preventing her from crumpling to the floor. Cora could see the tears running down her face, reflecting the very pain of loss she, too, was feeling. She looked over at Josephine, who was sitting beside Andrea. Josephine wore shades, but Cora still noticed the tears streaming down from underneath as she held her daughter Tracy's hand as if her life depended on it.

Cora realized this couldn't be easy for the two who had lost their husband/father and son/brother just a year before.

Her mind flashed back to the conversation, though brief, she'd had with her sister out by their old childhood swing only two days prior before she walked off.

"Now really isn't the time, but if you really must know, I'm not angry with you, Cora... I'm... disappointed."

Those words had filled Cora with so much guilt, compounded by Josephine's next statement.

"It was so hard for me after losing Charles and Nicholas. For months, I couldn't sleep or eat. I was operating on autopilot. I cried myself to sleep every night," Josephine revealed as a guttural sob slipped through her lips.

Cora had wanted to comfort her but knew it was better to let her finish.

"I wanted my sisters by my side... Andrea was there for a while, calling and checking on me, but then life got in the way, and the calls became fewer. I'm grateful for her support. I really am," Josephine murmured, gently bobbing her head.

"But I also needed my big sister."

Cora stood before her little sister with her mouth opening and closing, no sound coming out as her throat worked hard to produce sound. The guilt she felt grew into a crippling giant.

Cora felt so helpless. She wished she had the power to ease all their pain, to erase all of the bad that had happened in the past two and a half decades.

She turned back to the podium where her aunt stood, supported by Uncle Luke as she gave the eulogy. Both their eyes were rimmed red and full of tears.

After the final prayer was given for the family, they had one last chance to view their father's body.

This was it— her final goodbye to her father. Her heart was so heavy, so burdened, and barely holding up in her chest after she finally found the courage to look at him as he lay there in the coffin, looking so at peace as if he were only sleeping.

"Daddy..." she sobbed, turning away from him toward Josephine, who was the closest to her. She hesitated to reach out to her sister, whose entire body shook with her own sobs, but she realized that they both needed this hug more than ever, so she reached for her and pulled her into an embrace, holding her tightly. Josephine collapsed against Cora's body as her whole frame continued to shake from her cries.

"Shh, it's going to be okay, Jo." Cora comforted her sister even as her own tears continued to fall. Holding her sister's head between her hands, she raised her up from her shoulder to look into her eyes. "You're going to be okay, Jo. We're going to be okay." Cora didn't know how true that statement would be, but at this moment, she believed it with her whole heart.

Josephine nodded in thanks for the assurance as she went back to gripping her sister close to her. Cora looked over to see that Andrea had their mother in a similar embrace as she, too, sobbed uncontrollably.

They would be okay. They had to be.

Back at the house, Cora barely registered the persons coming in and out of the living room where they had gathered. They came with food, offered their condolences, and spoke highly of her father, but all Cora or any of the others were able to do was nod mechanically at the well-wishers and offer a "thank you" here and there.

Cora got up from the couch she sat on and made a beeline for the door, but she was intercepted by her mother.

"Cora," she murmured, her voice weak and still unsteady from her tears.

Cora turned toward her.

"I want you to meet someone," she said. With that, she

turned to a man Cora had never seen before. Cora took the time to look him over before introductions were made. The man had to be over six feet tall and filled out the charcoal suit he wore nicely, hinting at a very muscular frame. His black hair with hints of gray at the temples was neatly swept away from his oval-shaped face. He wore a distinct peppered goatee that framed his face quite nicely. If she guessed right, he was in his late forties or early fifties.

"Cora, this is Jamie Hillier. He's worked with your father over the years. He's the one who remodeled the barn into the restaurant for us," her mother informed her.

The man looked at her with a hint of recognition in his coffee-colored eyes. Cora was baffled as she was sure they had never met before now.

"It's nice to finally meet you in person. Your father has spoken about you a lot."

Cora was surprised by that statement. Brushing it off, she reached out to shake his extended hand.

"It's nice to meet you, Mr. Hillier. Although I can't say I've heard about you before now, I'm sorry." Cora gave him an apologetic smile as she released his hand.

"That's okay," he assured her.

"I like what you did with the old barn, though. I was truly impressed by the entire design," she appraised his work.

"It was all your father, actually," he corrected. "I just followed his vision to make the masterpiece that Willbery Eats is."

Cora gave him a polite smile, not knowing what to say to that.

"If I may say so, your father was a great man; fair and—"

Cora accidentally snorted at the statement.

The short pause from Mr. Hillier suggested he had heard the unseemly sound that escaped her lips. She anticipated the awkwardness that was sure to follow.

"He was kind, compassionate, and I really enjoyed being his contractor. I haven't had a client quite like him in a while," Mr. Hillier continued to say, choosing to ignore her faux pas. She was grateful for his discretion, although she did see the slight grimace from her mother, which suggested the sound hadn't gone unnoticed by her either.

After thanking Mr. Hillier for his kind words about her father, Cora finally made her escape outside to get some well-needed fresh air. She was confident everyone was inside or on the front porch, so she went to the back.

The evening sun was setting quickly. The skies were bathed in the brilliant orange and pink hues of its final spectrum of rays dispersing over the horizon.

She heard the door open but didn't bother to see who had come through it.

"Hey," she heard her sister say.

"Hey, Drea," Cora replied, using her nickname. She turned to face her, leaning her back against the rail.

"Dad must be cheesing up there in heaven," Andrea stated, pointing at the sky. "Seeing so many people come out to celebrate him." She lightly bumped Cora's shoulder with her own as she leaned against the railing of the back porch as Cora was doing.

"He always was the life of the party," Cora joked.

It was no secret that their father had loved the spotlight just as much as he had loved showing off his daughters' athleticism and intelligence. They were all usually in the top three high achievers while going to school. All in all, they were an all-American family wrought with their own brand of chaos that had eventually ripped the family apart.

"What happened to us, Cora?" Andrea asked after a while of them just leaning over the railing.

Cora turned her head to her sister, noting the troubled look etched on her face. She sighed as her shoulders slumped, not knowing how to respond to her sister's question. She wasn't sure what she wanted her to say.

"When you left, I felt so alone." Andrea began to open up to her.

Cora felt a pang of guilt— she had been feeling a lot of those lately.

"You never came home, and I felt lost. The letters you sent just weren't the same as talking to you like we used to. I struggled to write what I wanted to tell you, so I just stopped writing anything meaningful. It wasn't like you were coming back even if I begged."

Cora turned to Andrea, saddened by how her leaving Oak Harbor hurt her and Josephine so much.

"I'm so sorry, Drea. I never meant to hurt you. I just didn't know if I would be welcomed back after everything Dad had said— all the threats. I was young and naïve. I know that doesn't excuse my actions, and if I could take it back, I would," she spoke earnestly as she looked at her sister.

"I know that wasn't your fault, Cora. I realize now it would be unfair of me to blame you for something you had no control over—"

Cora sensed the *"but"* in her statement.

"What is it, Drea? You can tell me," she encouraged.

With a sigh, Andrea straightened up and slowly made her way to one of the two chairs. Cora waited.

"You remember when I came to see you in Cali after leaving here?"

Cora racked her brain, trying to remember what had happened when Andrea had shown up at her room in the middle of the night in her third year of college.

"You told me to go home, that you couldn't worry about school and me at the same time. You said I had a better chance of working at the inn than bumming it." She filled in the blanks for her.

Cora felt the guilt dig even deeper into her barely sutured heart. From Andrea's perspective, she realized how hurtful those words had seemed at the time. In truth, she was only trying to protect her sister, not wanting her to suffer as she had been doing because her father had cut her off completely. She had wanted her to be sure of her decision to leave and to have a well-thought-out plan that could sustain her living away from home.

"Andrea, I'm really sorry for what I said and for how I made you feel. At the time, I was trying to protect you."

Andrea looked at Cora with a perplexed expression, causing Cora to explain further.

"I didn't want you to struggle like I was struggling. Dad cut me off when I left, and I was barely making ends meet. I had to pick up extra shifts at work just to pay for the heat in the apartment. I was living off ramen noodles and crackers, for god's sake. I didn't want that life for you, and at the time, I just thought it would have been better for you to go back home at least until you had a plan."

Andrea nodded in understanding, but her eyes were somber.

"I wish you had told me this that day, Cora. Maybe then, I wouldn't have—"

"Wouldn't have what?" she prodded.

"It doesn't matter now." Andrea waved off the question.

For the second time in the past two days, Cora's heart broke as she looked at her sister, completely helpless.

61

Chapter Eight

The repass was finished. Everyone had given their final words of condolences before departing. The only people left in the house were family members.

Cora looked around at everyone as they either sat in the available seats in the room or stood around conversing with each other. The scene triggered nostalgia from simpler times— when they used to gather like this to celebrate Thanksgiving, Christmas, and birthdays. In those settings, her father was very much the key to those gatherings. He had been the patriarch, after all. Now his death became the catalyst that brought them all back together.

She was happy to see Uncle Luke's children, some of her first childhood friends because they all had been so close in age and the closeness of their family. Even though they had been close when they were young, years and distance had affected their relationship as well.

Nevertheless, she was happy to catch up with them before they had to separate again. Kerry, the youngest, had left immediately after the funeral, but Charles and Tessa, the twins, and

Brian had remained. She'd learned that Charles and his wife, Sharon, ran a successful law firm here in Oak Harbor and that Tessa was the head nurse at the local hospital. Brian worked for the city. A few of their children had been at the funeral but had left right after the ceremony. Cora was sorry she and her girls hadn't gotten a chance to acquaint themselves with them. Aunt Stacy's children had left immediately after the funeral too.

"Cora," her mother said, bringing her out of her thoughts.

Cora looked at her mom, eyes questioning.

"Mr. Wilson says we should come to his office at ten o'clock tomorrow for the reading of your father's will," her mother informed her.

Cora smiled and then nodded. "Okay, Mom."

The following morning, Cora, her mother, and her two sisters sat in the office of their father's lawyer and executor of his estate.

"Let the record show that this is the Last Will and Testament of Mr. Samuel Arthur Hamilton that was amended six months prior to this date," Mr. Wilson stated. "Also a matter of public record."

Cora felt her mother shift beside her, and she looked over to see her anxiously wringing her hands that sat in her lap. Andrea's and Josephine's stoic expressions gave no indication of their feelings.

Finally, she fixed her eyes back on the middle-aged man who was about to provide them with the details of their father's wishes.

"I, Samuel Arthur Hamilton, being of sound mind, do declare the details contained in this document to be true and in detail express my full intention in the matter of how my personal possessions, properties, and effects would be divided at the time of my death."

Cora suspected that her father would not have left anything much to her and thought it a mistake to have come to the reading as all that the lawyer would be presenting today, she could have a copy of later. She chalked up her presence here as an act of support for her mother and sisters.

Cora surmised she could do without any of the accumulated funds and property as she wasn't lacking anything. She still had a good-paying job, a house, and a sizeable savings if she found herself in dire straits.

She was surprised by the revelation that her father had so much equity he was able to split his life insurance policy in a way that saw her and her sisters receiving ten percent of the total sum and their daughters each receiving fifteen percent. The rest had gone to their mother, which was foreseeable. A few personal effects were left to Uncle Luke and Aunt Stacy.

"The Willbery Inn, Willbery Eats and property in its entirety, I leave to my three daughters: Cora, Andrea, and Josephine Hamilton on the condition that they do not attempt to sell or dissolve it—"

Cora was taken aback by the revelation. Her mouth opened and closed as her eyes shone with the shock she felt. Looking over at her sisters, she realized that they had broken character and their faces likewise registered similar expressions of surprise.

Cora never expected her father to include her in the ownership of the inn, not after never having spoken to him about it for more than twenty-six years. This was—

"You must also commit to living in Oak Harbor simultaneously or taking turns to care for your mother and run the business until her death."

This was the final crux of his will.

"I don't understand," Cora finally spoke after a pregnant pause by the lawyer.

"Mom?" Cora turned to her mother, needing to know why that last part was a stipulation.

Becky looked at her daughter with guilt and sadness as she continued to pull at her fingers.

"Mr. Hamilton suspected that should this day come, Mrs. Hamilton would find it difficult to explain her sickness," Mr. Wilson said.

Cora looked back and forth between her mother and the lawyer, completely perplexed, her sisters exchanging looks of concern.

"Mrs. Hamilton has Amyotrophic lateral sclerosis, ALS. She only has a few years to live."

The news hit the sisters like a nuclear bomb.

"Wha-What are you saying?" Cora asked in disbelief. Her mouth felt as if someone had stuffed it with cotton, her heart beat loudly in her ears, and her palms began to sweat. She felt the room spin and then slow down as if she were in a nightmare that wouldn't stop.

"Mom... tell me this isn't true, that this is some sick joke," she heard Andrea's voice laced with fear and anxiety.

"I'm sorry, honey. I wanted to tell you all sooner, but-but Sam, he didn't want to worry you," their mother cried in anguish.

"How could Dad do this?" Cora finally found her voice. She felt her anger level rise. How could he have prevented them from knowing this life-changing news about their mother?

"I'm sorry, Cora." Her mother reached over to grab her hand in earnest. Her grasp felt stiff, weak, and so feeble. How had Cora not noticed this before?

"Girls, I'm so sorry." She repeated her apology to Andrea and Josephine.

"It's okay, Mom," Cora said. "Everything will be okay."

Cora squeezed her mother's hand reassuringly as she thought about the promise she had made to Josephine. She didn't know how they would do it, but they had to make it work for their mother. Time had literally been shortened.

After the final terms of the will were read, the ladies stood from their seats and shook Mr. Wilson's hand in gratitude. They turned to leave the office.

"Cora," he called out before she could exit.

Cora turned to look at Mr. Wilson expectantly as he came from around his desk to stand before her. "Your father wanted me to give you this letter. It's for you and your sisters to read."

Cora took the envelope from him and looked at it curiously before fixing her eyes back on the man.

"Do you have any idea what it's about?" she asked.

"No," the man replied, shaking his head.

Cora looked back at the envelope. "Thank you," she finally said before slipping through the door.

What could her father possibly have written? Why was it addressed to all three of them?

Cora made her way toward the parking lot where her sisters and mother waited for her. Andrea and her mother sat in the back of the vehicle, but Josephine stood on the outside, leaning against the front door. When she spotted Cora, she straightened up and made her way toward her before she could make it to the car.

"Cora, I need to talk to you," Josephine said as soon as she was in hearing range.

"Sure, sure." Cora nodded.

"Dad sure knows how to leave us rattled even from the grave," she blurted half jokingly, gaining a short chuckle from Cora.

"He was a complicated man in life, and his death would not be the exception." Cora sighed.

"Yeah, makes sense," Josephine agreed.

"I never anticipated that he would find a way to tie us to the inn like that."

Josephine smiled sadly. "That's what I want to talk to you about. I can't stay. I took a leave from work, and they're expecting me back in two days," she explained regrettably.

"Jo, it's fine," Cora told her reassuringly as she reached for her hand to give it a small squeeze. She was happy that after their last conversation, it seemed as if her sister was finally giving her a chance to make it right between them.

She knew there was still a long way to go, and her apology for not being there for her after the funeral of her husband and son had just been a Band-Aid fix. It would need a lot more conversations, acceptance of blame, and apologies from her to fix their relationship. She was still happy about the progress, though.

"We'll make it work."

"Thanks for understanding, Cora." Josephine smiled at her gratefully. Suddenly the smile dropped off her face. "I still can't believe that Mom has ALS. God, this feels like punishment." She drew in a long breath and then released it slowly.

Cora shared the same sentiment, but she had to be strong for the family. As the oldest, she hadn't been given a chance to be there for her family the way she would have wanted, but now she had the opportunity to do so, and she would not neglect it.

"I know. It feels so unreal." She looked back at the car with sadness. "I'm disappointed that they didn't tell us, but this is where we're at now. Based on what I know about this disease, Mom will need a lot of help and constant care as the disease progresses, and we have to be there for her."

Josephine nodded in agreement. "As soon as I can get some things in order, I'll throw in my support," she promised.

"Jo." Cora placed her hand on her shoulder to stop her. "It's fine. I don't want you to stress over this right now. We'll work it out."

Josephine gave her a grateful smile. The two made their way back to the car.

"Are you girls okay?" Becky asked when they entered the car.

"Yeah, Mom, were good. Don't worry about it," Cora tried to ease her mother's worry. "How are you feeling?"

She looked through the rearview mirror to see her mother look down at her hands guiltily.

"I'm sorry that you had to find out about my condition like that," she apologized again. "If I could give anything to reverse that decision, I would give it now." She looked up in earnest at each of her daughters.

"It's okay, Mom. We're past that. We just want to be there for you now to do what we can," Cora told her mother, trying to assuage her feeling of guilt.

"Yeah, Mom, we're here for you now. That's all that matters now," Andrea chimed in.

From the corner of her eyes, she saw Josephine reach up to swipe at her face. "It'll be okay, Mom." She spoke slowly, trying to conceal the slight tremble in her voice. Josephine turned her head toward the window. Cora suspected it was to hide the evidence of her tears from them and her heart constricted that much more.

Their mother started crying. "You girls are so good to me, and I know I don't deserve it."

Cora felt the wetness at the corners of her eyes and began to blink rapidly, refusing to let them fall as she started the engine and they made their way back home.

Cora now knew at that moment that this would be her home once again.

Chapter Nine

After dropping their mother off at home, the girls decided to visit one of the local establishments to get away from the house and the weight of events that were so fresh in their minds.

They found themselves at The Anchor, the local bar and diner back on SE Pioneer Way. Cora remembered the last owner to be the Smiths. Dad and Mr. Smith had been good friends. She wondered if they still owned the establishment and tried to remember if she had seen them at the funeral. Maybe she wouldn't have recognized them after so many years.

The first thing Cora noticed when they entered the establishment was the juxtapositioning of the bar and diner. She noticed it because the design was unique. The bar had high-back counter stools in a straight line along the long mahogany stained bar top. The blue and pink led lights were low wattage washing over the assortment of liquor bottles on the rack, the bar top, and stools in a way that made everything look colorful. The dining area was like a sunken lounge making the ceilings much higher and giving the space an airy feeling. The room was also well lit by low-hanging ceiling lights.

Cora made her way to the empty bar and took a seat in the middle. Her sisters sat on either side of her. The bartender, noticing their entry, had positioned himself, ready to take their drink order.

"Well, isn't this a sight for sore eyes," he cheesed. Cora looked at him, perplexed by his statement. "Triple H in the flesh."

At this, Cora squinted her eyes at him, trying to figure out whether she knew him. He did seem a little familiar, but she just couldn't place from where.

"Jack Fletcher!" she heard Andrea exclaim as if a light bulb had gone off in her brain.

Wait, it couldn't be...

"Oh, my god, Jack, I can't believe it." Cora broke out in a wide grin. Jack had been one of her good friends back in high school. They had run in the same circle, had the same set of friends, and went to the same parties. This Jack before her looked different from the Jack she knew back then, though. For one, he now sported a bald head and had the appearance of a bouncer with how bulked up he was. The only distinguishable feature that instantly sparked her recognition after Andrea's reveal was his friendly hazel eyes.

"What's it been, twenty years?" he asked.

"Eh, give or take a few years," Cora replied.

"I'm happy to see all three of you. This old place hasn't been the same since you guys left," he revealed.

Cora gave him a small smile.

"Where are my manners? What can I get you lovely ladies to drink?"

"I'll have a Giuseppe," Cora ordered. Her sisters gave their selection, and shortly after, they each had a glass of Reisling between their fingers.

"I'm sorry about your old man. He was a good one. I always admired his sense of purpose."

"Thank you," all three girls replied graciously, battling their own thoughts about their father.

"So you work here now?" Cora asked to change the subject.

"I own it," Jack corrected. "After a ten-year stint in the navy, I chose to come back here to set down roots. The Smiths were looking to sell because they were moving to Boca, and I had some cash saved, so I decided why not."

"That's great, Jack. I'm happy for you," Cora expressed sincerely.

Just then, another patron walked up to the bar and took a seat.

"We'll have to catch up some other time, ladies. Duty calls," he told them, moving toward the customer.

"Maybe we should head to one of the booths," Josephine suggested after a few minutes of them sipping and savoring their wine. The sisters all agreed choosing a booth in the back would provide the privacy they needed.

"I never did ask you what happened between you and Joel for you to be divorcing him," Andrea posed to Cora as they made themselves comfortable, offering bits and pieces of information about their lives outside of what was already common knowledge.

"Six months ago, I found out he has been having an affair with our housekeeper and that it went on for over a year and still is. When I confronted him to tell me the truth, he denied it, but then my friend called me and confirmed it." It still stung every time she thought about Joel's transgression. Sometimes, the pain wasn't as bad as it had been in the beginning— sometimes, it was just a dull reminder, and she was finding it easy to share the details with her sisters.

"Oh my god, Cora... that was a low blow," Andrea breathed out.

71

"It hurts more because I found out that after the divorce is finalized, he plans to marry her and move out to Florida."

"I'm sorry, Cora," Josephine gasped, reaching over the tabletop to rest her hand on top of Cora's as an act of comfort.

Cora flipped her hand to squeeze Josephine's in gratitude.

"It gets better with time." Her sister nodded in agreement.

"Still, it can't compare to the pain you've gone through," she commented, referring to the death of Josephine's husband and their seventeen-year-old son.

"I'm truly sorry that I wasn't there, Jo. I wa—"

"I know." Josephine let out a breath as she swirled her wine in her glass. "I admit I still cry myself to sleep some nights, but it's getting better. Some days, I fall asleep without the use of sleeping pills. I consider that to be progress," she revealed, looking up at her sisters, giving them the slightest of smiles.

Cora gave her a small encouraging smile, not knowing what else to do to ease her pain. Andrea rubbed her shoulders in comfort.

"My work as a sous chef keeps me busy— it keeps my mind off them. I'm trying to be strong for Tracy, but sometimes it feels like she's the parent and I'm the child. She took a year off from college to get her mind back in the frame of learning, she said. But I know partly it was because she's worried about me." Josephine smiled sadly. "Anyway, aren't you going to open the letter so we can see what Dad wrote?" she asked Cora.

She had forgotten the letter that sat in her handbag even though that had been the intention of coming here. Cora reached over and took the envelope from the confines of her bag. Carefully, she tore one end and removed the letter. She read it aloud.

Dear girls,
If you are reading this letter, then I suppose it means I'm

dead. What can I say that will make this moment much better for you all?

Firstly, I want you to know that I love each of you very much. I've never stopped. I know, in the end, it seemed like the opposite, and I am sorry for that. I was proud, selfish, and stuck in my old ways.

I held on to this anger and disappointment that should have never been directed at you in the first place, and it caused me to miss out on all your firsts after you left home. I missed your graduations, your weddings, the birth of my grandchildren. I missed seeing them grow up, hearing them call me grandpa.

I wanted to give you girls the world, but in the end, I nearly took it away from you. As I sit here writing this letter, my tears are flowing, and my heart breaks with the sadness I feel because of how I treated you.

The inn is yours— it would have always been yours even if you chose not to live here.

I know it might be hard to forgive me for my transgressions, but I hold out hope that you will find it in your heart to forgive me.

Please don't blame your mother for what happened. She loves you girls very much and has always defended you against my anger and stubbornness. I love her so much for being my voice of reason, for not being afraid to put me in my place when I was wrong— you just didn't see it, and I was so stubborn that it seemed as if she wasn't doing anything. I am grateful that she loved me through it all until I was able to accept what I had done. In all honesty, I didn't deserve her.

My wish is that you will take care of your mother, be there for her, and make her as comfortable as possible. She's the only woman I've ever loved, and this is my final act of love for her. If you choose to sell the property after she's gone, I understand.

Be good to each other, love each other and most importantly, stick together.

I love you all with every ounce of my heart.
Dad.

When Cora finished reading, not one dry eye was left in their booth.

"I wish I had come home even once just to let him know that I still loved him," Andrea sobbed. "Now, I'm not able to do that. Daddy's gone, and all I have in my heart is this hole filled with pain and regret."

The pain was palpable through the raw emotions she had just expressed, and Cora was right there with her. Her shoulders lightly shook as the tears continued to flow. She wished she had made it home too. She wished she had called him once in the past fifteen years— to let him know that she still loved him, that she needed her father.

"I picked up the phone so many times to call him after Charles's and Nick's funeral, but each time, I talked myself out of it. I wish I hadn't," Josephine confessed as her mascara formed dark streaks down her face, following the pattern of her tears.

Their father had indeed been repentant of his treatment toward them, but he was gone now. This only ripped Cora apart more as she imagined how close they had been to reconciling and the wide gap that would never be crossed now in this lifetime. He wasn't there for them to voice their acceptance of his apology and offer their own as they sought to move forward, to make new memories.

Her mind went back to his request on behalf of their mother, and in that instant, she realized she had to honor it. There was just no other way.

"I'll stay and take care of Mom and run the business," she stated out of nowhere. Her sisters looked at her first with disbelief, then relief.

"I don't have anything to go back to Seattle for anyway. I took a leave of absence from work for the next year, so I have the time to be here with her, and it will give me enough time to figure things out long term."

"I decided that I'm going to stay also," Andrea revealed. "The good thing about my job is I can operate my online business and write my blog pieces from anywhere, so relocating won't be a problem."

Cora was relieved that it wouldn't just be her there.

"That's great, Andrea. We need a plan of action. How we'll be doing this."

"Hold on, Cora," Andrea cautioned. "I do plan to be here, but not this week. I have to leave tomorrow for an important event that I'm hosting, but I'll be back in a week. This is possibly the biggest event of my career, and I can't imagine not attending." she explained.

Cora nodded in acknowledgment. "Of course. Okay."

"I have to leave tomorrow, too, but I'm going to try my best to get some time off from work. To be here," Josephine chimed in.

"Jo, don't stress it. We'll make it work."

Josephine gave Cora a grateful smile.

"Here's to us, the Hamilton sisters," Josephine declared, raising her wineglass, awaiting her sisters to do the same.

Cora smiled at the gesture of unity. She clinked her glass against Andrea's and Josephine's.

"Here's to the Triple H."

"Triple H."

Chapter Ten

"I'll call you when I get to New York."

"Okay, sweetie." Cora hugged her eldest daughter, Erin, and planted a kiss on her forehead as she prepared to see her off.

Erin turned to Julia, who gave her a tight hug. Julia had opted to stay an additional day before heading back to WSU to prepare for her finals.

"Call me," she said as she finally got into the back seat of Andrea's sleek army-green Jeep Wrangler.

"I'll see you in a week," Andrea informed Cora after a brief hug. She got into the driver's seat, and Rory waved to her and the rest of the family.

Josephine and Tracy were currently saying their goodbyes to Becky, then Jo gave Cora a brief hug and smile before getting into her own olive-colored Rav4. All three sisters had a penchant for the color green.

"Call me?" Cora implored her sister needing the affirmation that their talk, though brief and reminiscing over old memories, had started a new chapter in their relationship.

"I will," Josephine promised. Tracy hugged Cora and promised to call too before getting into the car.

Shortly afterward, both cars drove off, leaving Cora, her youngest, Julia, and Becky waving until they were out of sight. The three women made their way inside the house to prepare for the day.

Uncle Luke and Aunt Maria arrived an hour later to join them for coffee. They had left earlier in the morning to drop Aunt Stacy off at the assisted living facility back on Whidbey Avenue. She had suffered a stroke two years ago that had rendered her immobile. After many months of therapy, she had regained some functionality, but she still needed a considerable amount of help with her limited mobility. Her husband, James, had suffered a stroke just a year before her, but unlike her, he had died. She had agreed to go to the home, not wanting to be a burden to her children and family.

"Doesn't Aunt Stacy feel lonely, not being around family at the old age home?" Julia was asking her uncle.

"Oh no, she's quite fine. Ben, Rhonda, and the kids visit her regularly," Uncle Luke explained.

"Plus, she gets along quite well with the other residents. It's why she has a whole bridge team there."

"Oh, well, that's good to hear." Julia nodded her understanding.

"What about you, Julia? How is school going?" Becky cut into the conversation to ask.

Julia's eyes widened in surprise before they shuttered.

"School is... okay, Grandma," she offered, picking up a crumpet and stuffing her mouth.

Cora wondered what her hesitation meant. Was something wrong at school? She wanted to know, but this wasn't the right time to ask.

Not wanting her daughter to feel uncomfortable by the

conversation dwelling on her and school, Cora thought to change the topic.

"Mom, was Dad planning on doing work on the dock down by the harbor? I saw some supplies by the steps the other day."

Becky turned her attention to her daughter with a wistful expression.

"He was planning to expand the dock so that the boat could have a covered area, and there would be a raised area where we could sit and look out over the harbor," she revealed.

Becky shook her head in regret. "One of the many things he planned to do before…"

She gulped, unable to finish the statement. She reached for her coffee and took a sip while the table remained silent.

Cora realized too late that it probably wasn't the time to discuss the plans her father had before his death. It was still so fresh and too painful for her mother.

She was grateful for Aunt Maria, who once again jumped in to steer the conversation to safer waters.

"Did your mom show you the new blanket she knitted?" she asked Cora.

Cora was surprised to hear that her mother had actually made a whole blanket. The last time she had spoken to her mother about her knitting, she had lamented ever taking up the craft as nothing she tried to make ever looked like the design she started with.

"Really, a whole blanket?" Cora exclaimed.

"I had a little help from Maria." Her mother smiled in appreciation.

"That's great, Mom. I'm proud you didn't give up," Cora commended.

"Thanks, sweetie."

"I have an idea. Why don't we have dinner at the restaurant this evening? I would love to sample the food and get a feel of the operation," she suggested.

"That sounds like a good idea," Uncle Luke agreed. "I think it would be a nice gesture if we have Stacy there as well," he offered.

They all agreed it was a good idea, and Uncle Luke left the table to call Aunt Stacy to see if she wanted to come.

After coffee, Uncle Luke and Aunt Maria left to run a few errands, and Julia agreed to tag along, leaving only Cora and Becky at the house.

"I'm going for a walk in the garden. Care to join me?" Becky asked.

"Yeah, sure, Mom," Cora agreed.

Leaving the patio, they followed the stone walkway toward the garden. Two minutes later, they turned onto the path that led up to the wooden arbor adorned by the creepers that wound so intricately around the frame with a burst of vibrant, colorful flowers. Pushing the low gates, the two entered the garden. Cora gaped at the beauty of the entire setup. On either side of the path made by uneven stone slabs placed at equal distances apart with tufts of grass filling the spaces were the most beautifully lush and exotic flowers and ferns, the eyes could behold.

"Wow!" She was unable to hold back her wonderment at the display before her.

"This is just....wow." She turned to her mother, who gave her a knowing look.

"It is so beautiful," she affirmed. "Your father had the idea to do all of this for my fiftieth birthday, and every birthday since, he sourced a new species of flower to plant and surprise me with."

Cora was at a loss for words. She felt her eyes well with tears but held them at bay as she looked around. The love her father had for her mother was so palpable and, to be honest, so, so special.

Her heart constricted as she was transported into a memory of her father bringing home special little trinkets and souvenirs for her mother whenever he traveled. She remembered how her mother would beam at those little gestures and their long embraces and kisses that would have her and her sisters making gagging noises in fun. She had wanted to marry someone who treated her like how her father treated her mother, like how he treated her and her sisters before their falling-out.

Her mind then flashed to Joel and how different he had been from her father. She had loved him, and she knew he had loved her, but he wasn't a guy too sold on romantic gestures. He didn't like PDA, and flowers and gifts were mainly reserved for birthdays and anniversaries. If she were honest with herself, then she would have realized from the beginning that she was just settling, so desperate to find someone who was the complete opposite of her father personality-wise. She hadn't realized how much that had affected the progression of her relationship with Joel until now.

"I need to show you something," her mother said, inviting her to follow her farther down the path to an open space with a raised circular platform with garden chairs surrounded by pink and yellow chrysanthemums and peonies. As they came closer, Cora was bowled over by the beauty of the plethora of planted roses just behind the platform. She gravitated toward the solid and variegated hues of the whorled petals, her hand already out to delicately rub against the velvety surface.

She bent down slowly, breathing in the light perfume scents of the flowers.

"He worked tirelessly to make this all come together," her mother said from behind her.

"These are the last sets he planted." Her mother reached over to gently touch the bright orange roses rimmed by pink edges. She smiled with a faraway look as if reliving one of the many pleasant memories she's had with her husband.

Becky shook her head, turning to her daughter.

"He made this garden for me but also with the hope that

you girls would have made it home, and we could have cele-brated my birthday right here next year as a family."

Her mother's revelation surprised Cora. He had truly been making steps to reconcile, not just to have them realize his regret after he was gone.

Fresh tears rolled down her cheeks as she thought of how much she truly missed her father and wished they had been given the time to express their regrets and forgiveness. If she could rewind the hands of time, she would.

"He was so gutted by his decision to cut you girls out of his life. It drove him to work harder in making this place a dream," Becky declared, gesturing to the expanse of the property.

"He wanted you girls to be proud to call this place yours one day."

Becky came over and placed a comforting arm over Cora's shoulders. "I know what he did was wrong, and I'm not trying to excuse his actions, but I want you to know that he truly loved you all so much. When you left, Cora, it hit him really hard. He was angry and hurt, and he didn't know how to let it go. He took it out on your sisters, pushing them to learn the business and making them promise they wouldn't leave Oak Harbor."

The mention of her sisters' suffering because of her deci-sion made her heart that much heavier, but she knew the more significant damage had come from her becoming distant as she tried to make a life for herself, to show her father that she could have survived without him.

"In the end, it only drove a wedge in their relationship, and as soon as they were able to, they left the island."

"I'm sorry, Mom... for everything. I should have come home sooner. I should have told him that I still loved him. I sh—" Cora lamented as her voice broke off in a sob.

Becky pulled her against her chest, embracing her.

"He knew," she assured her daughter, which caused Cora to cry even harder.

After her tears had receded and Becky had wiped her own eyes, the two sat down on the garden chairs, spending close to half an hour talking about Becky's sickness.

Cora couldn't say she fully understood the progression of the ALS disease, but she was aware that at some point, her mother would lose all mobility, speech, and ability to breathe. She was scared for her mother. She wished there was more she could do, more studies that had shown promise in treating the disease, but she would do her best to be there for her mother, making her as comfortable as she possibly could.

After walking back to the house with her mother, Cora decided to walk over to the restaurant while Becky took a nap.

Cora played over and over in her mind the conversation she had with her mother about her disease as she passed the inn on her way to the restaurant. She needed to make an appointment with the doctor to determine if all treatment options had, in fact, been exhausted. She was so preoccupied with her thoughts that she had missed the other person coming toward her on the path.

Cora bumped into a hard, unmoving surface, losing her balance and falling backward, but before she could collide with the ground, a pair of hands securely wrapped around her arm and waist, bringing her up.

"Are you all right?" the deep baritone of a man's voice asked. The voice sounded familiar.

Cora looked up into the dark eyes of the contractor her father had hired to improve the property. He looked down at her with concern etched on his face.

"Yes. I'm fine," she replied, stepping out of his grasp. "I wasn't looking where I was going. Sorry about that," she apologized.

"That's okay," he assured her with a bright smile. "I wasn't paying attention to my surroundings either."

Cora gave him a grateful smile.

Chapter Eleven

"M r...?"

"Hillier, but you can call me Jamie."

"Okay, Jamie, I guess it's only fair you call me Cora then."

Jamie gave a slight bow of his head in agreement.

"Are you here to see my mother? She's actually taking a nap right now," she informed him.

"No, I came to see you, actually." Caught off guard, Cora's eyes widened in surprise at his statement.

"I called earlier today, and Ms. Becky told me that you would be in charge of the inn and any contracted work to be done," he explained.

"Oh," she simply replied.

Jamie scratched the back of his neck before he spoke.

"Um, yeah, so your father contracted me to expand the dock for his boat and also to build a gazebo at the back of the inn. I wish I could hold off coming to you, considering everything, but I have other engagements, and I just need to confirm whether or not you'll be going ahead with it," he dragged out, placing his hands in the pockets of his jeans, anticipating her response.

"Oh," Cora replied once more, seemingly unable to form a coherent sentence. She tucked a strand of hair behind her ear, trying to figure out what to say.

"I'm sorry, Mr. Hil— Jamie. I wasn't aware that there were other projects other than the dock expansion Mom told me about," she finally managed to answer.

"Yeah, there are a few more projects that we'd discussed but for a later date. The gazebo and dock were meant to be completed before the beginning of summer," Jamie explained.

"Which gives you approximately two and a half months." Cora nodded in understanding.

"Okay, I mean, you and my father already decided on the projects, and I suspect you had a good working relationship with him. I don't have any objections to you going ahead with the work," she assured him. "What do you need from me?"

"Were you headed to the restaurant?" he asked, looking from her to the direction of the restaurant and back at her.

Cora was surprised by the question but found herself answering. "Yes, I wanted to speak with the chef about the menu for this evening. We have a reservation, and I wanted them to prepare one of Mom's favorite dishes."

"Okay. Do you mind if I join you? We could get coffee afterward and discuss the plans," he offered.

"That sounds reasonable," she agreed, giving him a quick smile.

"After you." Jamie gestured. Cora walked past him, and he fell in step with her.

She was utterly in love and charmed by how captivating the structure before her was with its rustic exterior; its architecture disrupted only by the expansive transparent windows on either side that offered a slight view of the interior.

Jamie pulled out Cora's seat, pushing it back in after sitting down, then took his own seat. Shortly after, one of the waitresses Cora met earlier came to take their order.

"I'm sorry for your loss." Jamie expressed his condolences as soon as the server left to get their coffee.

"Thank you," Cora spoke as a small smile flitted across her face.

"If it's any consolation, I want you to know that Mr. Hamilton was a great man, and I truly admired him."

Before she could respond to him, the server arrived with their coffee.

"Thank you. It's Suzie, right?" Cora asked.

"Yes," the girl beamed, her already rosy-looking cheeks brightening with delight that Cora had remembered her name.

Cora gave the blond-haired girl a warm smile before turning and leaving, her feet bounding across the floor with renewed purpose.

She turned her head to see Jamie looking at her, his expression unreadable. Self-consciously she looked down into her lap before lifting the mug to her lip and taking a sip.

"My dad and I haven't seen eye to eye in a long time, but I remember that he'd always acted fairly with those he partnered with or worked for him."

Jamie shook his head in agreement, bringing his own mug to his lips to sip coffee.

The rest of the time was spent discussing the gazebo and the boating dock plans. Cora felt reassured that Jamie was the right person to continue working on improving the property. He spoke so passionately about what he would do, and at times, Cora was lost to the construction lingo, but she was intrigued by how animated he was. She needed the distraction from her pensive thoughts, so she didn't stop him.

"So, how long have you lived on the island?" she finally asked one of the questions she was dying to know.

"Born and raised," he beamed, leaning back in his chair.

"Really?" she asked, shocked by his response.

"I'm surprised we've never met. When I lived here, that is."

"That means Whidbey isn't as small as everyone believes. I actually lived in Langley from birth until I was eighteen. I left to go to college out of state after I graduated high school. I didn't plan to come back to live here, but then my mom got sick, and I made the decision to be there for her. I've never left since," he revealed, the brightness in his brown eyes dimming as his face took on a faraway look.

She wanted to ask if his mother was okay now but thought it would be too intrusive.

"When I started my company some twenty years ago, Langley was too small, so not much was going on there, building-wise. I chose to establish a presence here in Oak Harbor, and I moved here shortly afterward," he continued, keeping the topic away from anything too deeply personal.

"And how long have you known my father?" Cora asked him.

"I've known Mr. Hamilton for over fourteen years. We first met when he was looking for a contractor to build the restaurant. We immediately hit it off. He liked my discipline and fairness, and I liked his vision and no-nonsense persona. I've been on retainer ever since."

After the meeting with Jamie, Cora had a talk with Chef Daniel, who, to her delight, had the ingredients on hand to make the dishes she wanted.

It took Cora twenty minutes to make it to the house. She'd stopped to have a brief talk with Marg about the upcoming reservations. There were currently three occupants at the inn, but the number was expected to double by the end of the week as an additional three more guests would be arriving. Marg informed her that she would need to introduce herself to them as one of the new proprietors of the business.

Cora, upon entering the house, went to check on her mom, who was still sound asleep. She went over to her and could see the tired lines around her eyes even while she slept. She reached out to gently smooth her fingers over the worry lines that wrinkled her forehead. She placed a light kiss on her mother's forehead before exiting the room.

There was still time before the others made it back and before they needed to get ready for dinner, so she decided to take a short nap.

"We have pan-fried sea bass with lemon garlic sauce, roast leg of lamb in trotter sauce, and for sides, we have an airy carrot soufflé, green beans with sautéed onions, and za'atar bread crumbs." Pat, one of the servers, stood by their table reciting the main courses, all of which Cora had requested they make.

"Wow, I haven't had sea bass in a while." Her mother marveled at the choices available.

Cora was happy to know that she would be able to enjoy this meal. Perhaps it would take her mind off her sadness being surrounded by family and good food.

"I'll take the sea bass and a side of green beans and sautéed onions." She heard her mother tell the redhead, who had her pen and paper in hand, diligently taking their orders.

Cora took the roasted lamb along with Julia and Aunt Stacy, and the others had the sea bass.

"So Cora, what do you think so far? About the inn and restaurant, I mean," her uncle asked as all eyes were now fixed on her.

"It really looks amazing, to be honest," she admitted. "I know I haven't been back here in so long, but the work that has been done is truly remarkable."

"I agree," her uncle affirmed. "Sam's love for this place

made it what it is today. I'm glad he chose to stay and take over while I went away to fight in the war. If it wasn't for his steering, I don't think there would have been a property to come back to."

Cora smiled knowingly. Her father was nothing if not an astute businessman— an attribute that he was being praised for by those who did business with him. Her mind flashed to Jamie Hillier and the almost reverence with which he spoke of her father.

Shortly after their meal arrived, the conversation died down, and they all dove into their food.

If she hadn't been paying keen attention to her mother, Cora would have missed the slight wobble of the fork in her hand as she tried with great effort to get the food into her mouth.

"Mom, are you all right?"

Becky looked toward her daughter with panic written across her face, but she quickly masked it with a small smile.

"Yes, sweetie, I'm fine," she declared.

Cora slowly nodded, although she wasn't convinced.

The conversation around her picked up again, but all of Cora's attention was focused on her mother, who she could see was having a hard time grasping the fork. She wanted to offer her help, but she knew that would only make her mother uncomfortable.

Becky looked around the table as if to make sure no one was witnessing her misfortune, and Cora quickly averted her eyes before she could see the sadness that had crept up at her inability to eat properly. She didn't want to embarrass her any more than she knew she already was.

Suddenly there was a loud clatter, and they all turned to the source of the noise. Her mother's fork lay face up on the plate with bits of food still attached to the end while the remaining particles were scattered away from the plate on the table.

Cora looked at her mother to see her eyes glistening with unshed tears as her right hand fisted on the table.

"Mom," she exclaimed, rushing to her side. "How can I help, Mom?" Cora rushed out, still confused about the symptoms of the disease.

Becky didn't answer, but a fresh stream of tears flowed down her cheeks as she kept her eyes lowered.

Cora reached for her hand and gently massaged her stiff fingers as she tried to get them free from their tight hold.

"I'm sorry," her mother cried. Cora's tears threatened to make an appearance, but she knew now was not the time; she needed to be strong for her mother, to let her see that she was capable of taking care of her.

"It's fine, Mom," she soothed, reaching up to brush her free hand against her mother's cheek, which was clammy to the touch. "It's not your fault. We'll get through this." She brought her mother's hand to her lips and kissed her knuckles before giving her a reassuring smile.

"Everything is going to be okay."

The rest of the family chimed in, stating they dropped their forks all the time, trying to lessen the severity of what had happened. Finally, the family decided to end the evening so that Becky could get some rest. Uncle Luke and Aunt Maria gave her a hug and spoke words of comfort to her before they left with Aunt Stacy.

Cora led her mother upstairs to her room and helped her undress before securing the covers around her.

"Get some sleep, Mom. I don't want you to worry about anything. I'll take care of everything," she promised.

Before Cora could turn to leave, Becky reached out to her daughter with her functioning hand.

"Thank you, Cora," Becky spoke in only a whisper.

"I love you."

Her heart broke at the tenuous state her mother was in. There had to be another alternative to this. Something the doctors hadn't tried.

There had to be.

Chapter Twelve

"Is Grandma okay?" Julia asked Cora as soon as she entered the kitchen. She had just left her mother's room and went straight to the kitchen in need of a glass of wine.

Julia sat on the barstool around the island with a glass of juice in her hand.

Cora saw the genuine concern in her daughter's eyes, and she felt guilty.

"Sweetie, there is something that I didn't tell you about Mom. I only just found out myself, but I should have said something." Cora sat on a stool on the opposite side of the island as she prepared to tell her daughter the news she was having a hard time accepting.

"Jules, Mom has ALS... what you saw this evening was a symptom of the disease, and it's only going to get worse from here on out," she confessed.

Her daughter looked at her, shocked by the news.

"What are you saying, Mom? Worse how?"

Cora released a heavy sigh as she reached across the tabletop to grasp her daughter's hand.

"It means over time, Mom will lose all mobility, her ability to speak, and worst-case scenario, she'll lose all ability to breathe on her own."

"Oh, my god, Mom, that is awful!" Julia exclaimed, perturbed by what she was hearing. "Poor Grandma... she just lost Granddad, and now this."

Cora gave her daughter's hand another squeeze before releasing it.

"It's very rough on Mom, but now is the time we have to be there for her more than anything. Dad's gone—" Cora paused. It was still so painful each time she brought up the fact that he was no longer with them.

"It's up to us to keep her healthy, to make her feel loved and not alone," she finished, lips pursed inward.

Her daughter gave her a sympathetic smile.

"Julia, I've wanted to ask you something since this afternoon," Cora spoke slowly as she stared intently at her daughter, gauging her reaction.

Julia's eyes widened slightly, then they shuttered as she looked down at her hands now clasped in her lap. Cora could see she already knew what her mother was about to ask her.

"Is something wrong at school?"

"School's great, Mom." Julia brushed off her mother's concern with a short unnatural laugh.

Cora's heart clenched at her daughter's attempt to appear okay.

"Julia—"

"Mom, just... drop it, please? Everything's fine. I'm just having a bit of a problem with a few of my courses. It's no big deal. I'll be fine. I just need to study harder, that's all. My midsemester exams are just around the corner, and I was feeling a bit overwhelmed, but when I get back to campus, I'll hit the books hard, I promise," Julia rushed out. "I'm not even planning on taking a spring break."

Cora sighed as she leaned back on the barstool, her body slightly arched over the low curved back of the chair, and looked at her twenty-year-old daughter. She knew Julia wasn't being completely honest with her. Whenever she was caught off guard, she tended to ramble, skirting around the real problem.

"Julia, I understand it must be overwhelming for you, considering all that has happened this year, but I don't want you to think you can't talk to me about what's bothering you. I'll always drop everything to listen and help you. You're my daughter, and I only want what's best for you," Cora shared, willing her daughter to feel the sincerity of her words.

Julia gave her mother a lopsided smile while her eyes barely registered the action.

"Thanks, Mom, I know you'll always be there for me, and I love you for it, but... I am fine." She enunciated every syllable of the last three words.

Leaning forward, Cora reached out and moved a few strands of brown hair behind Julia's ear before she cupped her cheek lovingly.

"I love you, too, honey, and I know you're strong. Just don't be too strong that you can't burden me," Cora pleaded. Raising herself off the stool, she placed a chaste kiss on her daughter's forehead before straightening up.

"I'm going for a walk. Would you like to join me," she offered, hoping her daughter would say yes.

"I think I'll sit this one out."

"Okay, sweetie." With one last look at her daughter, Cora headed for the front door and stepped out into the cool spring air. The sun had set a few hours ago, but the sky wasn't pitch black. Instead, it was littered with stars, and the full moon had cast shadows over the landscape and further illuminated her path. She pulled the sweater tightly against her body as the cold air sought to penetrate her frame.

She had witnessed one of her mother's episodes in just over a day since receiving the news of her diagnosis. Cora was sure there had to have been many more incidents like that within the six months in which she had been diagnosed, but tonight had been scary. She didn't know what she was expecting. Her mother had expressed that her ALS progression was quick, but Cora had been caught off guard to witness it like that at the dinner table.

She considered how taxing the care of her mother would be later on, but she had committed to the task. She was just happy that at least one of her sisters would be there to help her over these hurdles to come.

Cora felt herself hit a hard wall, and she began to go down when a pair of hands reached out and pulled her back up as it had earlier in the day.

"We have got to stop making these accidental meetings a habit." She heard the humor in Jamie's voice and looked up to see that it was indeed him. She could clearly make out his face in the glow of the moonlight— enough to see the twinkle in his eyes as they crinkled at the sides and the smirk she was sure he wore.

"I'm sorry about that. You seem to always catch me off guard," she admitted. Realizing his hand was still holding her waist, she took a few steps backward, and he released her.

"What are you doing here?" she asked, genuinely curious.

"I came to drop off a few supplies," he volunteered. "I'm planning on starting work on the dock tomorrow."

"Oh, that sounds great. You weren't lying when you said you worked on a schedule," she joked, flashing a smile.

"When it comes to my work, I never joke," Jamie said seriously. "So where are you off to?" he asked her, giving her a quick once-over.

She still had on her cami midi white floral dress partially covered by the green sweater and strappy dress sandals, an ensemble she had put together for her dinner at Willberry Eats.

"Just out for a walk," she told him simply with a slight shrug of her shoulders.

Jamie looked her over once more. She was happy that the moonlight wasn't as luminous for him to see the slight flush of her cheeks at his glance. She wasn't sure why she felt self-conscious by his inspection of her outfit.

"I'm going for a drink and some good old hometown karaoke by 'The Anchor,' care to join me?"

Cora looked at him, taken aback by his boldness. She wasn't sure it was a good idea, and she didn't want to give him the impression that she was interested in offering anything past a platonic relationship. She opened her mouth to decline the offer, but he beat her to the punch.

"I'm not inviting you out on a date," he clarified as if he had read her inner thoughts. "You just look like you could use a drink and maybe a change of scenery."

As he spoke, his hand came up to rub at his neck. That was a nervous tic of his, she realized.

"Besides, you're too dressed just to be going for a stroll," he finished, giving her a toothy grin.

She should say no, but he was right. She needed a change of scenery, with the weight of the disastrous dinner this evening and the helplessness she felt, not being able to get her daughter to open up about what was bothering her still fresh in her mind — if only just to forget for a short time, she knew she needed this.

"Sure, why not?" she agreed, receiving another wide grin from Jamie.

Cora went back to the house to let Julia know that she was going out for a while with the contractor and that she would be back before midnight.

She rushed to explain, *"It's not a date,"* after seeing the shock on her daughter's face.

"Does he know that?" her daughter asked, arching an eyebrow. She could hear the skepticism in her voice.

"Of course he does," Cora assured her. "I'll be back soon." She walked up and gave her daughter a tight hug.

"Be safe," Julia called after her.

Jamie met her by the entrance in his Ford F-150 truck. She was happy he had turned on the heat, which hit her body in a pleasant way after the coldness of the air outside.

Fifteen minutes after leaving Willberry, they were at the bar.

The bar wasn't crowded, and she was happy about that. She went and sat on one of the unoccupied stools while he excused himself to retrieve the wallet he'd forgotten in his truck.

"Hey, Cora, how are you?" Jack came up to her immediately after spotting her.

"I'm okay, Jack." She plastered a smile on her face. "I just needed a night out," she explained.

"You here with your sisters?" he asked while polishing the shot glass he held in his hand.

"No, they had to leave. I'm actually here with a contractor my father hired to do some work at the inn," she explained.

"You're talking about Jamie Hillier, right?"

"Yes. How do you know him?" she asked.

"Jamie is good people. He actually remodeled this bar for me," Jack revealed.

"Wow, it seems he has been doing a lot of work around the town," she marveled.

"Yeah," Jack agreed. "He's actually one of those contractors in high demand here on Whidbey Island."

Cora nodded in appreciation.

"Hey, Jamie." She heard Jack greet the man of the hour as he sat on the empty stool to her right.

"Hi, Jack, how's the family?"

"Janice is great, the twins are a handful, but that's what you get with teenagers nowadays."

"Janice?" Cora asked disbelievingly. "Janice Bigny? You married Janice Bigny?"

"Yes, I sure did," Jack beamed with pride.

Cora remembered back in high school that they never got along. They ran in the same circle of friends, but they were always at each other's throats and tended to avoid each other. To find out they got married was a real shocker.

"Wow." Cora exhaled, unable to find any other word in her vocabulary to express her incredulity at the news.

"Turns out all that bickering back in high school was a ruse to hide our true feelings," he joked. "I can't imagine ever marrying anyone else, though," he confessed seriously.

"I'm happy for you two. I truly am. It's just unexpected. But wow, congratulations and twins, that's wonderful."

Jack beamed with pride.

"What can I get you two to drink?" he asked, looking between the two of them.

"I'll have a whiskey sour," she ordered.

"Just a club soda," Jamie said from beside her. "Designated driver."

Jack went over to the stacked racks to throw together Cora's choice of drink and poured a glass of club soda for Jamie before moving on to another patron who had signaled him.

Cora took a sip of her drink, enjoying the tartness of the lemon and the sweetness of the syrup blend that tamed the bitterness of the whiskey. It was refreshing, and she was glad she had chosen to come out tonight.

Feeling eyes on her, she turned to see Jamie looking at her with an unreadable expression.

Chapter Thirteen

A week had already passed, and a lot had happened. Julia went back to college, and Cora had accompanied her mother to two doctor's appointments to discuss her illness and adjust her medication and therapy sessions. Two more guests had arrived at the inn, and the restaurant had been fully booked twice over the weekend, causing her to jump in to help the waitstaff.

Between caring for her mother and running the inn and restaurant, she was exhausted and felt stuck in a whirlwind. Andrea had called two days ago to inform her that she would be arriving today. Cora was elated for the extra help that her sister would provide because she truly needed it.

Cora sat in her father's office, going over the numbers. So far, the net income of the inn and restaurant was favorable; there were only a few creditors, and the inventory of all assets and supplies looked great. Her father's records were well detailed, which meant she had little reason to question her mom or the staff to fill in the gaps.

There was a knock on the door, startling her.

"Come in," she instructed.

"Hey," Jamie greeted her as he stepped through the door. His frame was slightly taller and more solid than her father's as it filled up the opening. "Do you have a minute?"

"Sure, come in," Cora told him, packing up the ledgers and putting them aside as Jamie fully stepped into the office.

"I wanted to know if you have a preference for the type of wood I use to frame the gazebo," he asked.

He and his crew had shown up the day following their time at the bar. They had started to fit together the platform for the extension of the dock. Jamie had explained that they would be using aluminum pipes to secure the deck before putting up an additional frame to build a double-decker dock upward.

"What are the options?" she asked, removing her reading glasses.

"Cedar, rosewood, and spruce wood," he listed.

Cora thought over the options, not knowing what the difference in each was.

"Which one would you choose?" she asked.

"Well," he stated, "all three are great choices, but in terms of durability, cedar is moisture and decay-resistant and repels insects." He gave her his professional opinion.

"Cedar it is, then," she affirmed.

"That's a cute picture," Jamie stated, looking behind her.

Cora turned to the picture in question. It was a picture of her and her daughters at Victoria Falls in Zimbabwe. Erin had just entered her teenage years and was going through the awkward phase of her body and emotions changing. Joel, on her request, had planned an African Safari tour, and the view and splendor of the falls had been the icing on the cake of one of the most beautiful trips they had ever been on.

"Those are my daughters," she explained. "You briefly met Julia." She pointed at the younger-looking girl beaming from ear to ear in the photo. "And that's Erin."

Erin's face was the total opposite of her sister's as she looked into the camera with a slight, shy smile on her face.

"They're lovely girls," he complimented.

"Thank you," she humbly replied. "What about you?" she asked. "Any kids? Wife?"

"Yes, actually," he revealed, reaching into his pocket to take out his wallet. Slipping it open, he reached into one of the compartments to take out a small square photo that he held before Cora's face.

"This is Lily," he proudly beamed as he brought the picture closer for her to see.

The young girl with raven-colored hair smiled unashamedly back from the photo.

"She's beautiful," Cora expressed.

"Just like her mama." Jamie smiled sadly down at the photo before him.

Cora gave him a questioning look, which prompted him to explain further, "I lost my wife three years ago to leukemia."

"Oh no, I'm so sorry, Jamie." Cora's heart went out to the man before her as his usually confident persona looked so broken talking about his deceased wife.

"It's fine. It gets easier. I can't say I don't miss her, but I'm learning to be happy again, to cherish the memories we made together, specifically our daughter," he spoke.

Cora nodded her head in agreement. She wanted to give him a hug, but that would be crossing an imaginary boundary that she didn't dare step over.

"So what about you? I know about your girls, but you've never once mentioned your husband." Jamie gestured to the simple gold wedding band she still wore on her ring finger.

Cora looked down at her hand, feeling a tug at her heart at what it would signify once she stopped wearing the one piece of jewelry that retained some semblance to her old life.

"I don't because... we're getting divorced," she replied simply, keeping her eyes averted.

"His loss." She heard Jamie say nearly under his breath as if he hadn't intended for her to hear him.

"So I believe we've shared enough of the heavy stuff for one day. I'll order the cedar so my men can start putting up the frame," Jamie spoke, rising to his feet.

Cora was grateful to him for not prying. The topic of her husband was still a sore spot for her that she hadn't even discussed with her mother. That was the last thing she wanted to talk about.

"Great, as soon as you get the quote, just let me know so I can put in a money order," she informed him.

Jamie gave her a smile and a slight nod before heading for the door.

He paused before exiting. Cora waited for him to say whatever it was that had him opening and closing his mouth several times as he nervously rubbed the back of his neck.

"Have a good day, Cora," he finally spoke, his voice almost pleading.

"Thanks. You, too, Jamie," she replied sincerely.

After Jamie's departure, Cora spent the next half hour making a list of things needed for the inn and restaurant. When she made her rounds, she would add any other items the staff would notify her were needed.

Andrea arrived in the afternoon. Becky had eaten her lunch and went to take a nap.

"How was your event?" Cora asked her sister after helping her with her luggage.

"It was great," Andrea beamed. "Nerve-racking but a complete success. I received quite a number of offers to help some large companies create content for their website, run their advertising and social media pages," she continued.

"That's wonderful, Drea," Cora cheered, her smile wide

with how proud she was of her sister's success. "I am truly happy for you."

"Thanks, Cora." Andrea smiled. "Where's Mom?" she asked.

"She went to take a nap. Since switching medications, she tires easily," she explained.

"What are the doctors saying?" Andrea asked, squaring her shoulders in preparation for the news.

"They say she's one of the lucky few because there are some new experimental drugs on the market that may be able to help slow the rate of neuron deterioration," Cora replied with a slight shrug of her shoulders. "It's still touch and go, though."

Andrea sighed as she plopped down on the bed in her old room on the ground floor. "Well, I'm at least happy that we have some time with her."

That was the only consolation they had in this situation. They had learned of their mother's illness before it was too late for her to communicate with them, to spend time with them without outright feeling like a total burden.

"Have you heard from Josephine?" Andrea asked Cora.

"Yes, she called twice last week. She spoke to Mom, and we spoke too. She said she had something to tell me but that she couldn't do it over the phone," Cora revealed.

"Okay, sounds serious." Andrea furrowed her brow.

"Yeah, that's been my thought since her call," Cora agreed.

"I'm going by the inn to have a talk with Marg. Want to tag along?" Cora asked her sister.

"Honestly, Cora, I'm still beat by the number of activities I've done this past week, so I'm going to take a nap. When I'm fully rested, you can bring me up to speed," Andrea stated, running a hand through her long dark locks.

"Yes, of course. Get some rest."

Cora left and made her way toward the inn. She took her

time making sure to admire the surrounding vegetation and landscape on her ten-minute walk. The sun was high in the sky and highlighted the beauty of nature. The low-cut emerald-green grass that spread across the expanse of the property and was interrupted by trees and colorful flowers growing out from the earth was truly magnificent.

Cora stepped through the double mahogany doors of the inn and made her way over to Marg Lewis, who was speaking with a female who wore a blond pixie cut with her back to her. She looked to be in her late twenties or early thirties.

"Cora, just in time," Marg spoke, flashing her a wide grin. The female whose back had been to her faced her now with wide eyes as if in recognition.

Cora found it odd as she couldn't remember ever meeting this young woman before.

"Cora, this is Selina, one of our guests. She thinks she knows you," Marg informed her.

"Oh..." Cora gave Marg a questioning look, but it was the woman who spoke next.

"Mrs. Avlon, we've never met formally, but I am a huge fan of your work," the woman explained, grinning from ear to ear.

Cora was relieved that the woman wasn't someone she had met before and had forgotten about.

She shook the woman's outstretched hand.

"Welcome to Willberry Inn, Selina. It's a pleasure to have you here," she greeted her.

"The pleasure is all mine, Mrs. Avlon," the woman continued to beam.

Cora bristled at the use of her married name. Pretty soon, she would be referred to only by her maiden name.

"I'm sorry for fangirling so much. It's just you inspired me to follow my dreams of becoming a journalist," the woman revealed.

Cora was truly surprised by the revelation.

"Your piece on expressing yourself even when it's unpopular to the masses helped push me out of my comfort zone. I now have a blog and over fifteen thousand subscribers."

Cora was surprised and touched that this woman had that much respect for her work. "That's wonderful, and thank you."

After her meeting with Marg, she made it back to the house. It was eerily quiet, and she suspected that meant that both her mother and sister were lying down.

Cora found herself in the kitchen. She had planned to make chicken Alfredo, asparagus, and Caesar salad for dinner, so she got the ingredients from the refrigerator and began prepping for the meal.

"Need some help?"

Cora jumped in surprise, turning with the knife clutched tightly against her chest to see her mom standing at the entrance.

"Mom, you scared me."

Becky walked over, displaying a lopsided smile.

"I'm truly sorry, Cora. That was not my intention," her mother apologized.

Becky went to the sink and washed her hands while Cora turned back to cutting the chicken into the desired portions.

"Need any help?" Her mother repeated the question from earlier.

"It's fine, Mom. I've got this," she assured her, briefly looking up from her work to give her mother a smile.

The knife froze in her hands as she noted the look of disappointment on her mother's face.

"Mom, what's wrong?" she asked.

Becky sighed, and she looked at her daughter with sad eyes.

"When I agreed not to tell you girls about my diagnosis, it was partly to avoid being treated like this— like an invalid," her mother expressed, the sadness in her voice gripping Cora as a wave of guilt washed over her.

"I'm sorry, Mom. I don't want you to feel helpless. That's not what I'm trying to do for you. I just thought you could relax and watch while I prep, that's all. I'm sorry. It won't happen again," Cora apologized. "Can you get the tray of eggs from the fridge for me, please?" she asked in an attempt to appease her mother.

Becky agreed and went over to remove the tray while Cora continued to mince the seasoning.

A moment later, Cora heard the tray fall and the cracking of eggs as they hit the floor before she looked up to see her mother's hand twitching and desperate tears in her eyes, ready to fall.

Chapter Fourteen

It had been almost two weeks since Andrea's return to Oak Harbor. Cora was happy for her presence, especially with how frustrated she felt some days. Those days when her mother could barely move her right leg, and the fingers of her right hand curled under. Cora spent over an hour those days massaging her mother's leg and her hand while slowly straightening her fingers.

She would look up at her mother and catch the look of helplessness displayed there before she gave her a small smile to mask it.

"Cora, I have an idea," Andrea suggested to her sister as they sat out on the patio, enjoying the sun's warmth.

Cora looked over at her sister, waiting for her to finish.

"We haven't gone out on the water since we've been here. Why don't we take Dad's boat and head out of the harbor for some sightseeing? We could maybe go for a swim in Skagit Valley after," she proposed.

Cora looked at her sister's hopeful face and caved.

"Okay, but only after Mom goes down for her afternoon nap."

"That's perfect." Andrea smiled warmly, pleased with the plan.

* * *

Tiny water droplets spattered Cora's face and body as the boat glided effortlessly over the sea. With Andrea at the steering, Cora took the time to admire the turquoise waters as the sun glimmered off the surface. This far out from land, the view of the mountains was even more magnificent. Cora had seen a few harbor seals but no orcas. The boat passed along the coast of the Camano Islands and the many private homes scattered along the waterfront.

"Wow, I can't believe how much I missed being out on the water," Cora said to her sister, who turned to give her a knowing smile.

"It truly is beautiful out here," Andrea replied, her eyes closed and chin tilted up toward the sun. A moment later, she said, "I'm going to bring the boat around the south side. I want to take a dip where the water is warm."

Cora nodded her head in agreement wanting to immerse herself in the warm waters as well. After mooring the boat, the two sisters removed the beach dresses they had worn over their swimsuits and made their way to the steps leading down into the water.

As she immersed herself in the water, Cora welcomed the warmth that seeped into her body after the slight chill from the windy ride. Kicking her feet out, she went onto her back and began to float, looking out at the clear blue skies looking back down at her.

Andrea swam up alongside her and mimicked her actions.

"Let's not wait twenty years to do this again," Cora heard Andrea say from beside her.

"Definitely not," she agreed.

"Cora?"

"Mm-hmm?"

"I really missed you," Andrea confessed.

Reaching across to grasp her sister's wet hand as they remained afloat, she gave it a tight squeeze.

"I missed you too, Drea. I'm really sorry that I hurt you. If I had known, I would have—"

"Cora." Her sister halted her speech. "It wasn't your fault. I should have listened to you and come back home, but I was just so stubborn and wanted to prove you all wrong."

Turning over and treading water, Cora went over to her sister, pulling her up and hugging her body to hers. The two embraced for a good half a minute, without any words, each drawing warmth and strength from the other.

The two sisters swam back to the boat and used the gallon of fresh water to wash away as much of the brine from their skins as they could. Cora applied sunscreen to her body, and Andrea did the same.

Not wanting to head back to land just yet, they lay on the boat's deck, soaking up some Vitamin D from the sun.

"When I left your apartment, I went to New York to stay with Amanda."

Cora turned to her sister, who had her hand shielding her eyes.

She didn't speak; Andrea needed her to listen— the journalist in her knew that, and as her sister, she knew that.

"Amanda had a nice apartment her parents were paying for, and she was enrolled in NYU."

Cora remembered Andrea and Amanda had been good friends back in high school before her parents moved to New York in the latter part of her sophomore year.

"She didn't have a problem with me staying with her, and I gladly took the offer because I wasn't planning on coming back here."

Cora reached over and gave her sister a light squeeze on her shoulder, letting her know she was still there, listening.

"After a time, though, I felt like a bum, that I needed to start making plans for my future. I saw this ad for a new hire for a private catering company, so I applied, and I got the position. I liked my job because the pay was good, and I was able to help with getting groceries for the apartment. It's the least I could do. And I enrolled in community college. I was so happy," Andrea expressed. "Knowing that Dad wouldn't have the final word, I wouldn't have to hear him say, *I told you so*. My life was back on track. But then I—"

Cora watched her sister struggle to finish the story. She could see the tension that tightened her facial muscles. Cora reached over and cupped her cheek in an act of comfort.

Andrea finally removed her hand from her eyes and looked up at Cora with sadness.

"I made so many mistakes, Cora," she lamented.

Cora knew she was talking about her pregnancy and Rory's father. Talking about it was causing her so much pain.

"Drea, it's okay. You don't have to finish the story now," Cora soothed. "I'll be here whenever you're ready," she promised.

Andrea reached over and squeezed her fingers while giving her a grateful smile.

Cora sucked in a deep breath before exhaling, and then she began to say, "At the beginning of our separation, I blamed myself for the failure of my marriage with Joel. I thought maybe I hadn't been doing enough to keep him interested, and I started drinking more than I ever had in my entire life. I almost became an alcoholic," she confessed with a shudder as her mind went back to the dark days.

She felt Andrea put a comforting hand on her back that was turned to her.

"It got better, though. I was able to pull myself back together and not feel like my life was teetering out of control. But it still hurts, knowing I spent nearly half of my life with the same man, building a home, a family, believing we were so in love and that we would grow old together. Instead, he's living with our housekeeper playing house... waiting for the divorce to finalize so he can run off and marry her." Cora released a mirthless laugh.

"I'm sorry, Cora," Andrea murmured, coming up to wrap her arms around her sister's torso while resting her head between her shoulder blades. "Joel is a fool to throw away two decades of marriage like that. He will regret what he did, but it will be too late," Andrea assured her.

Cora rested her hand on the arm around her waist and gave it a grateful squeeze. "We'll get through all of this, Drea. We have each other now," Cora assured her sister.

The two sat in each other's arms in comfortable silence as the waves gently rocked the boat back and forth.

"Let's head back, I'm starving after all that swimming and sightseeing, and it's getting late."

Cora stood to her feet and reached out to help her sister up.

The sisters docked the boat when they arrived at the harbor and made their way toward the house.

"Cora!"

Cora turned toward the voice and saw Jamie taking determined steps toward her.

"I'm going to head inside and see if Mom is awake," Andrea informed her, discreetly giving Jamie a once-over. Cora raised her eyebrow questioningly at her sister, not sure why a smirk had appeared on her lips. Andrea walked toward the house, not offering any hints.

Cora turned to the man who stood towering over her five-foot-five frame.

"Jamie, hi, what's up?" she asked.

"I wanted to show you something. Are you busy?" he asked, looking behind her to the house where her sister had disappeared.

"Not necessarily," she replied, wondering what was so urgent.

"Shall we? It's over by the inn," he informed her.

Cora fell in step with him as they made their way toward the inn.

"It's not in the inn," Jamie explained with a grin, stopping her from walking toward the front of the inn.

She looked up at him, perplexed.

"Here, come with me," he offered, taking her hand in his without thought.

Cora looked down at their connected hands and to the back of his head, surprised. She followed him mutely, not sure if she should remove her hand from his or allow him to continue holding it to take her to whatever it was that he wanted to show her.

They walked about two minutes away from the inn. Jamie released her hand when they came upon the gazebo in the finishing stages. She marveled at the beauty of the structure. All the lines were clean, and the intricate handcrafted patterns at the top accentuated the high ceilings well. Cora especially liked the maze pattern of the brick walkway that led up to the gazebo, where she also saw that the pattern had been carried all through the entire structure.

"Wow, this is—"

She couldn't finish her statement, but her face revealed how astounded she was by everything. The level of workmanship was excellent, even for a simple structure as a gazebo.

Cora turned to Jamie and was caught off guard by his eyes already focused on her.

"Do you like it?" he asked, his hands deep in his jean pockets as he waited for her to respond.

"I love it," she assured him with a grin. "My father was right to hire you. You truly are an artist," Cora complimented.

"I aim to please, madam." He grinned, showing off his straight white teeth before doing an exaggerated bow.

Cora laughed at the silliness.

She found herself getting into the act and, without hesitation, curtsied.

Jamie laughed a deep belly laugh that shook his frame and triggered the muscles in her own face to relax into a wide grin.

"Thank you for that," Cora said, placing her hand on his arm.

"Anytime, milady." Jamie smirked.

Cora headed to the house, thankful for the laugh Jamie had drawn from her with his theatrics. She could definitely see them becoming good friends.

Cora made it up the steps to find Andrea sitting on the porch swing in a daze. There was a mixture of pain and sorrow etched across her sister's face that concerned her. She could see that her eyes were rimmed red and that she'd been crying. Cora took a few strides toward her sister and sat next to her.

She had no idea what was wrong, but she was about to find out.

Chapter Fifteen

Cora spent the next hour listening to Andrea lament about not telling Rory about her father and deliberating whether it was a good idea to do so now that she had just learned of his passing. She knew her sister needed a supportive person, someone to listen to her as she tried to unravel all her thoughts until she could come to a solution she thought made sense. She was happy to be that for her.

Their mother had left for the inn to visit with one of the guests, who it turned out was the daughter of one of her oldest friends.

"I'm so lost." Andrea sighed, frustrated as she paced back and forth by the kitchen island.

Cora glanced up from thinly slicing the rolled-up pasta dough she had before her. She gave her sister a small sympathetic smile.

"It's your choice to make, Andrea. It might not be the easiest one, but only you can make it. No matter what the decision, though, I'm always here for you." Cora comforted her sister.

"I know," Andrea acknowledged. She came around the island and gave Cora a hug from behind, resting her head on her shoulder.

Cora warmed over at her sister's action.

"Need some help?" Andrea asked as she continued to cut the pasta strips.

"Sure. Can you get the rack, unravel these, and hang them to dry?" she asked, pushing the rolled-up strips she'd already cut to the side.

"Sure thing," Andrea agreed, removing her arms from around her sister and doing what she asked.

The two worked in silence for the next fifteen minutes. When the pasta was finally added to the boiling water and the sauce was simmering, they sat on the stools on the other side of the island.

"So, what's going on with the contractor?" Andrea asked with a mischievous glint in her light blue eyes.

The question caught Cora off guard.

"What do you mean?" she asked, not sure what answer her sister was looking for.

"Oh, come on, Cora. You can't tell me you haven't taken notice of what a handsome specimen that man is?" Andrea raised her brow, all the while smirking knowingly.

Cora wasn't sure she liked where the conversation seemed to be heading. Still, she entertained her sister.

"I mean, he isn't bad to look at," she spoke flippantly, shrugging her shoulders.

"Just to look at?" Andrea probed, head tilted back, eyes squinted, and a purposeful smile as she waited for Cora to answer the question.

Cora frowned. The conversation was heading toward dangerous waters.

"Yes." She drew the word out slowly. "He is nice to look at, and he is an employee." Cora made sure to put extra emphasis on the latter part of her statement.

"Oh, you're no fun." Her sister pouted like a child.

Cora laughed at her antics.

After her laughter had died down, she asked, "What do you want me to say, Andrea?" Her eyes were questioning. "I'm in the process of getting a divorce." The weight of the words falling from her lips was as real as the last time she had mentioned them.

"And?" Andrea turned fully on the stool to look squarely at her sister, her blue eyes searching Cora's, assessing.

Cora sighed. "I'm forty-five and getting divorced from a man I've spent half of my life with. I have two grown children, plus Mom's sick, and running the inn and restaurant doesn't give me room to think about dating anyone right now."

Cora got up from her stool, went to remove the pasta from the stove, and stirred the sauce one last time before turning the burner off.

"Cora," her sister said gently from where she sat.

"You deserve all the happiness in the world. I know it must scare you to think about ever giving someone a chance after Joel's betrayal, but everyone is not your ex, sweetie."

Cora turned to her sister and gave her a meek smile.

"Andrea, I know you're trying to make me feel better, and I appreciate it, but I just don't want to date anyone right now, especially since I'm still waiting on my divorce to be finalized. I don't know if I ever want to put myself in the position to..." Her mouth opened and closed, but no sound came out.

Cora couldn't finish the sentence. She knew how jaded it would have made her sound if she explained that she would never put herself in such a position to get hurt by a man again. She didn't have to say it, though. The sympathetic look in her sister's eyes told her she already knew what Cora had stopped herself from saying.

Before Andrea could say anything else, their mother walked into the kitchen.

"Hi, Mom. How was your visit to the inn?" Cora asked, tucking a strand of hair behind her ear.

"Oh, it was lovely," Becky beamed. "Kathleen is such a sweetheart. I hope you don't mind that I invited her to dine with us."

"Sure, Mom, there's enough food. She's more than welcome," Cora told her.

"Wonderful," her mother exclaimed. "She'll be here in the next fifteen minutes. Do you need any help?" Becky made her way around the island.

Cora exchanged a worried look with Andrea. She had told her about the incident at the restaurant and what happened the other day with the tray of eggs.

"It's okay, Mom. You should go wash up and prepare for your guest. We've got this," Andrea said as she stood from the stool and walked around to the cabinets to start removing the dinnerware.

"Oh... okay," Becky replied. The slight downturn of her eyes and the softness of her voice made it clear she was disappointed by their response.

"Oh, Mom, why don't you taste the sauce... see if it's okay?" Cora rushed to appease her mother's hurt feelings.

"It's okay, sweetie. I'm sure it tastes great," Becky insisted before turning away. "I'll just go wash up and wait for Kathleen to get here." With that, their mother left the kitchen with her shoulders slumped, head lowered, the total opposite of how she had entered the kitchen earlier.

Cora and Andrea sighed.

She knew their mother wasn't used to not being able to do things for herself, but it was also necessary that she gave up some of her autonomy, considering she wouldn't be able to do anything for herself very soon.

When Kathleen arrived, their mother made the introductions before they all filed into the dining room, which Andrea had already set up in preparation for the meal.

"Mom always dreamed of coming back here to live out the rest of her life," Kathleen told them while accepting the meaty sauce and scooping a generous amount over the pasta that was already neatly stacked on her plate. "Since her wish didn't pan out, I thought it was a good idea to honor it the best I can," Kathleen continued to say as she passed the bowl to Cora, who sat across from her.

"I am truly sorry for your loss, Kathleen," Becky spoke, reaching over to give the woman's hand a comforting squeeze. "Mary Ann was a sweetheart. I wished she had been able to move back here too," she continued to say. "It would have been like old times."

Cora noticed the faraway look in her mother's eyes and the smile that didn't meet her eyes.

Becky had explained to her daughters that Kathleen's mother had been a native of Oak Harbor but had left after meeting Kathleen's father and had only been back a handful of times until her death over two years ago. However, they had maintained their friendship over the years.

"Thank you, Mrs. Hamilton. I am grateful for your kindness," Kathleen spoke graciously to her.

Cora had caught the melancholy look in the other woman's eyes before she expertly masked it with a sincere smile and her light tone. She surmised her predisposition was a result of her profession.

"So, how long are you planning on staying in Oak Harbor, Kathleen?" Andrea asked.

"I'm not sure," Kathleen answered. "I actually took a leave of absence from work for eight months. I just needed a change of scenery— somewhere away from the hustle and bustle of city life, somewhere peaceful and less busy."

The women nodded their heads in understanding.

"I'm actually planning on fixing up the family home back on Koetji Street. It's been a while since anyone has lived there. I figure it might be in need of some major repairs, so I'm in the market for a contractor at this time," Kathleen revealed.

"Oh, well, I guess this is your lucky day. Cora can help you with that," Andrea spoke up, giving her sister a sly smile from across the table. "She's actually very close with one of the top contractors here on Whidbey," Andrea offered, her tone very suggestive.

Cora almost choked as a piece of pasta got lodged in her airway. Sputtering, she quickly reached for the glass of water. She gulped down the liquid in an attempt to displace the particle and breathe freely once more.

"We're not... we're not that close," Cora rushed to clarify as soon as she found her voice. "He's actually a contractor my father worked with and is still on retainer. I can't deny Andrea's statement about his skill, though— he is very talented. I can give you his business card if you'd like to use him."

"Oh yes, thank you. That would be a great help." The woman nodded her head gratefully.

Cora caught Andrea giving her a knowing look as her blue eyes continued to twinkle with mischief.

Cora narrowed her own gray-blue eyes at her sister, giving her a subtle shake of her head, *no*.

Andrea's light smirk transformed into a wide Cheshire cat grin, and Cora felt her anxiety slowly creep up.

She opened her mouth to say something Cora was sure would be controversial in its delivery, but there was a loud clatter before she could get the words out.

Cora turned to look at her mother, as did the others. Like at the restaurant, the fork had slipped from her hand and hit against the side of the plate as strings of pasta lay outside the plate, the white tablecloth stained by the spatters of sauce. Her hand was folded in on itself and stiff, but unlike the last time, there were no tears. However, her eyes remained transfixed on her hand on the table and her lips pursed. She recognized that her mother was embarrassed.

Cora slowly got up from her seat and walked around the table to kneel before her mother. She took the fisted hand in hers and gently massaged her mother's hand and fingers. She looked up, about to speak, but her words caught at the look in her mother's eyes as she looked down at Cora— it was one of shame mixed with the hint of hopelessness and defeat.

Cora's heart constricted as it had been doing the past couple of weeks.

"It's going to be okay, Mom," she soothed, continuing to massage her hand. Reaching up, she caught the single tear that escaped from her glistening eyes.

"We're all in this together."

Becky reached down her left hand and cupped her daughter's face tilting her head to look back at her. Her eyes still glistened with the unshed tears there, but Cora could also see the look of gratefulness.

"Thank you," she spoke with feeling. "I don't know what I would have done without you girls." Becky looked from Cora to Andrea, who was hovering on her other side. "Both of you are my beautiful angels."

Cora smiled up at her mother as Andrea rubbed circles on her back. They were oblivious to the fact that someone was at the table with them, their attention riveted on their mother. It was the clearing of a throat that reminded them of the presence of their guest.

Cora looked at Kathleen, who gave her an apologetic look.

"I can see that you probably need some privacy, so I'll just head back to the inn." She rose from her chair. "Mrs. Hamilton, it was an absolute pleasure to be here in your home," she said, giving Becky a warm smile.

"I'll walk you out," Cora offered.

Chapter Sixteen

A month had flown by as if it had only been minutes on a clock. The work on the gazebo was pretty much finished other than some minor things that still needed to be done, and the dock was near completion. Cora was pleased with the progression and made a mental note to thank Jamie for his hard work.

Kathleen had also hired him to fix up her family home that had passed down to her after her mother's death, and that work too was coming along well if she was to go by Kathleen's high praises for the man's work ethics and craftsmanship. It seemed she was taking a real liking to him. Cora didn't know why but it bothered her, especially whenever she would see them around the property talking and laughing, her touching his arm sometimes.

Cora saw them standing at the front of the inn as she walked by on her way to the restaurant to do her routine check. Jamie had his hands in his blue denim jeans and shook his head in agreement with whatever the blond-haired woman was saying to him. Jamie's eyes flicked from the woman to her, which caused a slight flutter in her chest. Cora raised her hand and waved in greeting, a small polite smile gracing her lips. Kathleen followed where his eyes were trained and, upon seeing Cora, raised her hand in greeting as well. She gave Cora a friendly smile which she returned.

Cora turned her head and continued on her way toward the inn. She didn't notice that Jamie's eyes remained on her a good twenty seconds after she had walked past the inn, but Kathleen had. She watched him stare at the daughter of her mother's good friend, and as if a light bulb had been turned on, her face lit up with a knowing smile.

Cora wasn't looking for a relationship. She didn't need one, not with the baggage she was lugging around. It was for this reason that she had tried to avoid Jamie as much as possible to prevent the seeds her sister had planted in her head from taking root and growing wild. She didn't need to add to what she had on her plate right now. Besides, her mother's health was gradually deteriorating, and she would need her undivided attention more than ever.

Becky could barely use her right hand. She had to train her left hand to do everything her right hand usually did, but the deftness of the hand was still far from perfect. Four times already in the past month, Cora or Andrea had to help her get into her clothes and help her button her blouse.

Cora didn't mind doing it for her mother, but every time she had to intervene to offer assistance, she would see the pained expression on her mother's face, which only served to prick at her heart. Some days all they got from her were a few sentences and a few, "I'm fine," whenever they asked her how she was feeling. She wished there was more she could do to help her mother.

"Ah, Mrs. Avlon. How are you?" Chef Daniel asked as soon as she stepped into the kitchen.

"Hi, Daniel, I'm fine," she replied with a bright smile. "I told you to call me Cora, though."

Daniel gave her a sheepish grin as he raised his shoulders with his arms facing forward, palms out.

"Force of habit," he conceded.

Cora gave him a wide smile as she walked past him to look around the kitchen. Everything was spotless, from the stainless steel countertops to the tiled floor. She walked over to the tall man standing in front of the industrial stove as he busily stirred a pot whose content she was not able to see.

Rick, the sous chef, looked over his shoulder at her with a grin before looking back at the pot he was tending. Without warning, he turned to Cora with the wooden spoon in his hand. It was lightly coated with whatever sauce he was making, indicating she should try a little. The slightly sweet, slightly spicy sauce was really good.

"Mmm, this is fantastic," she gushed as she enjoyed the sauce. "What's it for?"

"The main dish we're serving later," he replied, giving her a charming smile.

"You're not going to tell me what it is, are you?"

Rick turned to her and opened his mouth as if ready to say something, but at the last moment, his lips pursed as he drew an imaginary zipper across them.

She shook her head and laughed as she playfully pushed him.

"You're no fun." She pouted.

This was their regular routine. Whenever she would ask him what he was preparing, he would respond that she needed to stick around to find out.

This little game between them had been going on for some time now. She didn't mind it, though, because every time she was blown over by his ability to surprise her with his creations, it kept her wanting more.

As Cora opened her mouth to speak to her employees, the server on duty walked in. "Pat, I'm happy you're here. There is something I wanted to say to all of you," she announced to the curly brown-haired server with the large-framed glasses. "I'm thankful for all the work you've been doing," she complimented, speaking loudly enough for the two chefs who were busy with their preparations to hear. "I know my father— Dad would want me to show my appreciation for the hard work you all have been doing. The restaurant has been doing well. We're attracting many clients, and business has been good."

"That's because you have been so receptive to our ideas, and your input has made the difference," Chef Daniel spoke up, bowing his head to her in reverence.

She was touched by his statement, and she noticed the others must have shared the same sentiments as they too smiled and nodded their heads.

"Thank you. I'm so grateful for the faith you've all put in me." She looked at each of them, making sure they saw how grateful she was. "For that reason, I wanted to announce that I will be giving you all a raise. Pat, you can let the others know as I'm sure you'll see them before I do that their service is appreciated, and they will receive a raise as well."

All the faces before her lit up at her announcement.

"Wow! Thank you, Ms. Cora," Pat rushed out in pure joy.

"Pat, please, just Cora will do. When you say miss, I feel so old... like I'm in a wheelchair," Cora advised the young girl shivering in alarm at her own words.

After sharing the news with the restaurant staff and picking up the purchase order for the items that couldn't be bought fresh from the market, Cora left on her way back to the house.

"Cora!"

She turned to see Kathleen waving her over from the second floor of the inn. She waved back at the woman.

"Please, can you wait for me? I'm coming down," Kathleen begged.

"Oh, umm... okay," she agreed, wondering what the woman could possibly want from her.

"Thanks for waiting," Kathleen said to her as soon as she made it to where Cora stood waiting for her.

"Sure. What is it you need?" Cora asked.

"Oh, nothing really," the woman spoke up, confusing Cora. When she saw Cora's raised eyebrow and uncertainty written all over her face, she rushed to clarify, "What I mean is... well, what I wanted to ask is..."

Cora was getting even more confused as the seconds ticked on. *Why did the woman call her if she wasn't really prepared to speak with her?*

"Is something wrong with the room?" Cora asked, trying to figure out if it was a complaint she was trying to lodge with her.

"Oh no— no," Kathleen rushed out. "My room is really lovely. I love it. I wouldn't change anything about it."

"I'm glad to hear it," Cora replied, smiling.

"What I actually wanted to speak to you about was Jamie."

"Oh. What about him?" That was her automatic response as apprehension seized her heart.

"Umm... I know it might not be my place to say, but I know I haven't been here that long and..." Kathleen let out a nervous chuckle, finding it hard to say what she wanted to say to Cora.

Cora was nervous about what she wanted to say to her as well. Her palms had gotten sweaty, her blood pressure elevated, and it felt as if a tight fist had captured her heart, cutting off her oxygen, preparing her for the confirmation of what she had suspected. She waited for the woman to continue.

"If I am totally out of line, you can tell me," the woman rushed to say again after some time of Cora standing there waiting.

"Kathleen—"

"I believe Jamie is smitten by you, and if I'm not mistaken, I believe you may reciprocate those feelings but are trying very hard to ignore them," the woman rushed out, looking at Cora seriously.

Cora was floored by the woman's observations.

"Wh-what are you... why would you..." She trailed off, not able to get her brain to formulate a response or her dry mouth to function. Her brow furrowed as she shook her head, and she took a step back as her heart beat erratically within her chest.

Kathleen's perceptive gray eyes stayed trained on her as she struggled to get her mind to cooperate. She gave Cora a sympathetic look and a small smile before stepping forward and placing her right hand on her shoulder.

"As a psychologist, my training usually gets the best of me, and at times, I talk out of turn. I'm sorry for putting you on the spot like that. I hope I haven't brought more harm to this delicate situation," the woman apologized.

"No, no, it's fine," Cora spoke up after finally finding her voice. "It's just that you caught me by surprise. I actually thought you were going to tell me that you were interested in Jamie," she confessed. "I was prepared for that. I was planning to tell you to go for it."

"Oh, honey... I'm sorry if I gave you that impression," Kathleen spoke up, her cheeks tinted red from the embarrassment she felt. "He is a good man, but he's not my type. He's a little young for me. Also, I'm in a relationship. However, he's stationed overseas for an entire year, being an Army sergeant and all," she informed Cora. "So no, I am not interested. I realized that you might be interested and just needed a little push in the right direction."

Cora sighed. "Jamie is a great guy, but finding love is the furthest thing from my mind or priorities right now." Cora turned away from the woman who waited for her to continue. "My mom is not well. You saw that the night you came to dinner. She has ALS. My sister and I have taken on the role of caregiver, and it has been taxing physically and emotionally. Then there's the inn and the restaurant, and I have to be emotionally available for my girls," she rationalized. "Plus, I spent more than half of my life with one person, and now I'm in the middle of finalizing our divorce." Her shoulders slumped in defeat.

After a good thirty seconds of silence, Kathleen finally spoke up.

"Cora, I get it, believe me, you have a lot on your plate, but you have to make time for your own emotional well-being, too," she reasoned.

Cora felt the pressure of Kathleen's hand on her shoulder, prompting her to turn her head to look at the woman staring at her with understanding.

"I'm not speaking to you as a professional here," she expressed. "From one woman to another woman, I am saying don't make what has happened to you take away the possibility of happiness. I was married for fifteen years, and after my first husband decided he didn't love me anymore, I thought it was the end of my happiness, and my self-confidence was destroyed. I threw myself into my work and avoided social events because I felt as if all men probably saw the same things my ex-husband found to be wrong with me." Kathleen smiled wryly before continuing. "I forgot all about my training. I allowed the lies to grow and fester because I knew he was only projecting his own insecurities onto me. Then I met John, and I almost chased him away, but he was strong." Kathleen laughed and shook her head. "He persevered and became my friend. Then, he taught me how to be special again, how to accept love again, and I'm so grateful for that." The woman remained smiling as she was transported in time, reflecting on the man she spoke about with so much love and compassion.

Turning her eyes back to Cora, she spoke earnestly, "Cora,

I don't know you that well, and my assessment is inconclusive, but I want to leave you with this piece of advice... it's okay to be cautious, but don't let happiness pass you by because of someone else's inability to love you the way you should be appreciated and loved. I really do wish you all the best, my dear."

Seconds later, Cora watched as Kathleen retreated back up the stairs to her room. She had no words because she knew that everything the woman said was true.

Chapter Seventeen

Cora couldn't sleep. No matter how she turned or fixed her pillow under her head to get comfortable, sleep just would not come. Her mind was unsettled — going over the conversation she'd had with Kathleen earlier in the day. She knew she wasn't ready for a relationship but would it be such a bad thing to consider Jamie as a friend. She couldn't deny the fact that she liked his company and he was easy to talk to, but she was also afraid she would get too attached and become disappointed or heartbroken.

Cora recognized that sleep was nowhere near and that she didn't know if she wanted to chance even a friendship with Jamie, so she got up from her bed and made her way downstairs to make some tea. She hoped she still had some chamomile tea bags left because she really needed something to ease her mind.

Cora turned on the kitchen light and gasped in surprise to see her sister on the floor by the fridge with a tub of ice cream opened and the spoon suspended between her mouth and the frozen treat.

"Andrea, why are you sitting on the floor in the dark... eating ice cream?" Cora asked, confused by her sister's actions.

"Hey, Cora." Andrea sighed as she pushed off the floor and took a seat at the kitchen island. "I couldn't sleep," she replied as she made herself comfortable, lifting the spoon back toward her mouth before closing her lips over the sweet coldness.

Cora gave her an understanding smile as she made her way to take down the kettle from atop the rack and get a cup from the cupboard. She filled the kettle with water and placed it on the stove before turning to her sister.

"Couldn't sleep either, huh?" Andrea asked.

"Nope," she agreed. "My mind is holding me hostage." She grabbed a chamomile tea bag from the box and dropped it in the mug, followed by a spoon of stevia, before turning back to stare at her sister.

"Have you ever felt like you have everything you could ever want to keep you happy, but then one thing falls out of place, and it just throws everything else out of whack?"

Cora furrowed her brow at her sister's question.

"I'm not following," Cora expressed. "Are you happy? Is there something threatening that happiness?"

Andrea sighed as she scooped more ice cream and put it into her mouth. "I'm terrified to tell Rory the truth. It will absolutely threaten my relationship with her. She'll see it as I've broken her trust." Andrea's voice broke into a sob at the end of her statement.

Cora rushed over to her sister, enfolding her in her arms from behind. Andrea turned her head into her chest and sobbed.

"How can one wrong decision from so long ago have the potential to cause so much destruction with just a few spoken words?" Andrea continued to cry into Cora's chest, and she let her, ignoring the whistling kettle.

"The smoke alarm will be triggered," Andrea warned as the

shrill whistling of the kettle continued. She disentangled herself from Cora, giving her the opportunity to go turn off the stove. Cora poured the piping-hot water into the mug and brought it with her to set on the island as she took a seat beside her sister.

"Andrea, I know that you did what you had to do to protect your child, and I believe that if you're honest with Rory, she'll understand," Cora reasoned, finding it necessary now to encourage her to talk to her daughter about the past. "She loves you. It has only ever been the two of you. She might be angry at first, but she'll come around. She'll understand. You have to have faith in your daughter, Drea." Cora bumped her sister's shoulder and gave her a reassuring smile.

Andrea smiled through her tears, grateful for the encouragement.

"I love you, Cora," she spoke with sincerity showing in her glistening blue eyes.

Cora gave her a warm smile and a side hug.

"I love you, too, Andrea," she affirmed.

Cora reached for the mug and raised it to her lips, but her sister's next words halted her ability to taste the warm beverage.

"So what's got you so wound up that you couldn't sleep either?"

* * *

Cora sat in one of the bamboo chairs on the patio, taking in some of the sun's rays that seeped through the louvers of the sliding pergola roof. The dark shades she wore were perfect in keeping off the excess glare from her eyes. She was glad for the peace and quiet only interrupted by the sounds of nature— the raspy chatter or chirrup of the birds that would stop by occasionally to feed at the bird feeder a few meters away and the rustling of the tree leaves as the wind whistled by. She could just fall asleep to the ambiance, and that was the plan as her eyes fluttered closed.

A shadow fell over her, blocking the sunlight and forming a distinct dark pattern behind her closed eyelids.

"Hi, Cora."

Cora's eyes immediately flew open to focus on the man standing above her. Her heart skipped a beat, and her mind went blank for a few seconds as she struggled to form coherent thoughts.

"Hi, Jamie, how are you?" she asked, politely smiling up at him as soon as her brain cooperated and synced with her lips.

"I'm good," Jamie replied, reaching up to rub his hand across his nape. "You?" he asked in return.

"I'm fine," she replied politely.

"That's great..." Jamie trailed off.

Cora willed her mouth to move— to say something to break the awkward silence that ensued, but once again, her brain had lost all sensibility, and she stared up at him with a nervous smile plastered on her face, the turmoil in her eyes hidden by the dark tint of her sunglasses.

"Did I do something wrong?" he finally asked, breaking the silence and surprising her at the same time.

"What do you mean?" she asked carefully.

The man standing before her raised his hand to his nape once more as he looked at her carefully.

"Ah, could you remove your shades?" he asked. "I don't mean to offend you. It's just I appreciate being able to see eye to eye with the person I'm speaking with," he rushed out in anticipation.

"No, I'm sorry I should have removed them earlier." Cora reached for the handle of her shades and moved them from her face, leaving her bare to Jamie's piercing onyx eyes.

"That's better." He smiled at her, causing the sides of his

eyes to crinkle with the movement. Her heart fluttered within her chest.

"I knew we probably wouldn't have been best friends—females usually give their other female friends that title, but I thought we were at least becoming friends," he said, sliding his hands into the pockets of his denim jeans. Cora's eyes followed the motion taking in the veiny appearance of his well-toned forearms that ran all the way down to the back of his hands, disappearing into his jeans. "Therefore, I would like to know if I did something wrong. What did I do wrong, so I can fix it," he finished.

Cora gave the man before her an apologetic look as she stood to her feet, feeling at a disadvantage in her previous position.

"I'm sorry, Jamie, you are a great person... you didn't do anything wrong. It's me. I just—" Cora trailed off, not able to string the words together that wouldn't suggest she was purposely avoiding him.

"I want to show you something," he offered.

Cora looked at the man who still towered over her with apprehension.

As if sensing her hesitation, he rushed out, "I promise it won't be long, and it's something you will appreciate."

"Jamie—"

"It's by the docks. It'll be less than ten minutes," he implored her.

"Okay," she conceded, giving him a small smile of acceptance.

His face broke out into a wide grin as he gestured toward the path that led down to the harbor, allowing her to walk ahead of him.

When they finally made it through the thicket of trees and shrubs creating a wall around the property, Cora was met with the finished dock, and docked directly under the raised deck was her father's boat, freshly painted and sporting the words, ***Silver Bullet***.

Cora covered her mouth in disbelief as she turned toward Jamie with questioning eyes.

"How did you—?"

"That was one of the last things your father asked me to do," Jamie explained, taking a step closer to the boat.

Her eyes welled with tears, amazed that her father had managed to surprise her so much and melted her heart in death more so than he had while alive. A tear slid down her cheek as her heart became overwhelmed by the gesture and Jamie's role in making it possible.

"Did he tell you the story behind why he gave me that name?"

Jamie averted his eye from staring at the silent tears that were now running down her cheeks as they fell to the ground and disappeared into the tiny spaces between the sand particles. His hand twitched at his side as if he was struggling to keep it there.

"Oh, actually, yes..." He swallowed before continuing, "He told me that he called you his silver bullet because when you first watched the movie with him at eight, you told him that you would always be his silver bullet to chase away the darkness that brought the werewolves," Jamie revealed.

Cora smiled in fondness as the memory vividly played in her mind.

"From then, you guys watched the movie reverently every year like clockwork." Jamie smiled as he reminisced. "He told me that story at least fifteen times. Each time, he added a little more detail that he forgot to tell me the last time." Jamie looked at her as he dropped even more overwhelming news. "You were all he talked about most of the time. It's like I got to know you before even meeting you... well, the young you," he confessed.

"All this time..." Cora shook her head in utter shock. "All

this time, I thought he was too angry with me to even care what I did." She gave Jamie a grateful smile, though it was tinged with sadness.

"Thank you for telling me, Jamie. I am truly grateful." She raised her hand and touched his forearm in gratefulness as a slight smile graced her lips, this time reaching all the way to her eyes. At the gesture, Jamie's face lit up.

"I'm happy to know I could have brought some clarity and some closure to you," he said, his voice laced with tenderness as her hand remained on his arm.

Knowing the acts of kindness that her father had done in the months up to his death had warmed her heart. She had missed out on so much due to her stubbornness. Now it was time to make up for it.

Chapter Eighteen

"I miss the days when she was so little, you know? Back then, she would hang on to every word I said, and I was happy to be granted the opportunity to be her protector. But now she's engaged, and even though I think it's too soon— they're so young, I can't get her to see my reasoning." Jamie ran a hand through his hair.

Cora nodded in understanding as she listened to the man sitting across from her on the patio complain about his daughter's decision to marry her high school sweetheart. She knew this feeling of helplessness all too well— knowing that your children no longer needed you the way they used to when they were just kids. It was that feeling that had you up at night worrying about their safety, hoping they make smart decisions, and praying that you wouldn't get a call that something tragic had happened to them. It was that feeling that you know no matter how much you try to caution them, they wanted to make their own decisions— their own mistakes.

"So you think it's because you wished she would have

remained your little princess forever?" she asked, looking at him.

"She will always be my little princess," he answered instantly.

Cora smiled at this. She admired his love and commitment to his daughter. It was an admirable quality.

"I understand, but you have to give her room to grow and make her own decisions, to make her own mistakes, or you'll just drive her away," Cora cautioned him.

Jamie sighed, running his fingers through the thick stubble above his upper lip before sifting it through his salt and pepper beard. "That's the same thing Brooke used to say to me when Lily started dating, and I would play the tough guy," he revealed. "She would say, 'you need to give her space, let her make her choices, or else you might just push her into making bad decisions just to get back at you.'" He air quoted as he tried to mimic a high-pitched feminine voice.

Cora laughed at his attempt, and he joined in shortly after.

"When I ignored her advice, she always knew how to straighten me out." He smiled fondly as his eyes glazed over in memory.

"You still miss her," she stated, more than asked.

"I do," he expressed, head moving up and down in sync with his words. "But every day gets better. I honor her memory by continuing to move forward, so..." He trailed off with a shrug.

"I admire the love you shared with your wife," Cora confessed. "It's such a rare gift, and sometimes it doesn't last." She added as her mind went back to her own marriage, "Love can be such a fickle emotion; one minute it's all you can think about, and in an instant, you're filled with betrayal and questions."

"Your ex-husband?" Jamie asked, even though she was sure he already knew the answer to that question.

Cora looked at him but said nothing.

"That man must need glasses of the highest potency to have let you go without a fight. I can—"

"He cheated on me," Cora blurted, effectively cutting him off midsentence. Shock registered on his face as he looked at her in disbelief.

"On you?" he asked incredulously.

Cora nodded.

"Wow! Blind and stupid." He blew out his cheeks, shaking his head, bewildered by her revelation.

"That's not even the worst part." Cora laughed. "He cheated with our housekeeper. They were in a relationship for a whole year. I only found out because my best friend was a part of the committee investigating him for workplace misconduct, and she told me the same night I confronted him, and he had vehemently denied it." She reached over to the table and picked up the glass of wine she had only been sipping on until now. She tilted the glass back as the liquid disappeared between her lips until nothing was left.

She reached for the bottle to pour herself another, but Jamie reached for it at the same time she did and quickly pulled it out of reach.

"Hey, easy there, Cora. I imagine the pain is still fresh in your mind, but you can't let it control you," Jamie cautioned.

"But I haven't even gotten to the fun part of the story yet." Cora giggled, already a little intoxicated. "As soon as the divorce is final, Joel— I didn't tell you his name did I?" she asked, having a one-off tangent from what she had planned to share.

"No, you didn't," Jamie spoke slowly. "Here, drink this." He reached over and placed the cup of water in her hand.

"Thank you," she expressed, gulping down the water.

"Now, where was I?" she asked, tapping her finger against her chin in thought.

"Oh yes, as soon as the divorce is final, my dear Joel is planning to marry our said housekeeper and move to Florida to live a blissful wedded life."

After her admission, Cora looked down into the empty cup, unwilling to look at Jamie. She didn't need to look at him to know that he was probably pitying her.

She felt the warmth of his touch on her shoulder and looked up to see that he had come around the table to stand at her side she suspected to comfort her.

"I'll repeat what I said before, Cora," he spoke seriously. "He is blind and stupid."

She gave him a grateful smile.

"You are an amazing woman, an amazing person, Cora. Don't make his mistake be the reason you shut people out." Jamie held her gaze, and in that instance, it felt as if time had come to a standstill. Her heart beat erratically against her rib cage as his piercing dark eyes stared, unwavering as if he could see right through her soul.

"Cora!"

Cora jumped, surprised. The sound of her name being called pulled her out of whatever invisible aura had held them tethered to each other by their gaze.

She jumped to her feet a little too quickly, causing her to almost lose her balance, but Jamie was right there to help her, his sturdy frame steadying her.

"Are you all right?' he asked in concern.

"Yes." She smiled, moving away from him. "I think I might have drunk a little bit too much wine." She winced.

"You did." He laughed.

"Hey." She feigned offense, giving his shoulder a hard push. It was as if she tried to push a hard wall.

"So, does this mean you'll consider my suggestion?" he asked.

"I'll think about it," she promised.

Jamie gave her a small smile just as Andrea stepped through the back door onto the porch.

"There you are." Andrea sighed in relief. "I was beginning to wonder." She trailed off, and her eyes landed on Jamie.

Cora looked from her sister to the man by her side. Andrea's face broke out into a smile.

"Well, hello, Jamie. I didn't know you were out here," she greeted. She cast her eyes on Cora once more before looking back at him; the glint in her eye that always worried Cora was there.

"Hello, Andrea, how are you?" Jamie greeted, smiling.

"I'm great," she expressed. "Even more so with yo—"

"Why were you looking for me, Andrea?" Cora interjected. She was afraid of the direction the conversation seemed to be heading.

Her sister turned her brilliant blue eyes on her, that sparkle even more from the mischief that brewed in them.

"A package came for you," she revealed. "But that can wait."

Cora sighed, unhappy that her attempt to dissuade her sister from further embarrassing her with her suggestive undertones and questions had failed. When had Andrea become so bold? She still remembered the outgoing yet shy teen that wouldn't do anything without her prodding or approval back in high school. Back then, Andrea had been nothing if not careful with her words and actions. This Andrea was different; she was spontaneous, straightforward, and easily the life of the party. A lot truly had changed between them.

The woman looked down at the small coffee table that still housed the half bottle of wine and the two glasses they had been drinking from. Her smile grew even wider, which caused Cora to sigh internally as she waited for the onslaught of questions brewing at her sister's mischief.

"I'd best be going now," Jamie chimed in. Cora looked

toward him to see that his eyes were on her and shone with understanding. He gave her a comforting smile before Andrea's head turned to him.

Jamie made a show of checking his watch. "It's getting late. I have a supply run to make and some work to finish up, so I'll see you, ladies, another time," he explained, walking toward the side exit.

Cora waved goodbye, thankful for his ability to read the situation and offer a solution that would ease the chagrin she would have felt had he remained and Andrea said what she wanted.

"Bye, Jamie... hoping to see more of you," Andrea said sweetly, which caused the man to chuckle at the blatant meaning of her words.

As soon as Jamie was out of sight, Cora hit her sister's arm.

"Ow!" Andrea cried out, rubbing the area Cora hit her.

"What was that?" Cora hissed, slightly throwing her hands up in disbelief.

"What was what?" Andrea asked, feigning ignorance.

Cora blew out her cheeks in frustration and turned away from her sister.

"Oh, come on, Cora. You said last night you would consider giving the friendship a chance. I was simply adding my voice of approval," Andrea explained, coming up to stand beside her.

"Andrea, I said I would consider it; 'consider it' being the operative words," she stressed.

"Plus, the way you spoke made it sound like we were starting a relationship, and that just can't happen right now," Cora continued to explain to her sister.

Andrea eyed her unconvinced but chose not to say anything.

"Please, Drea, I'm just... I need you to tone it down a bit," she implored.

Andrea sighed before putting her arm over Cora's shoulders.

"Okay, sis... I can't say I agree with your choice, but I will respect it. Just remember this, everyone believes that you deserve to be happy. I know you deserve to be happy; I guess... when the time's right, you'll know."

Cora tilted her head to the side to look at her sister, a small smile gracing her lips. She couldn't deny the fact that their personalities had changed significantly by the experiences they'd had over the years; the absence from each other's lives had left them close to being strangers. Yet the moments they'd had since coming back to Oak Harbor seemed to have narrowed that gap, and they could pick up where they had left off— they could be sisters again.

She reached over to brush some of the brown tendrils of her sister's hair away from the side of her face before leaning over to place a gentle kiss on her cheek.

"I love you, Drea."

Andrea squeezed her shoulder in acknowledgment.

"I love you too, Cora... always and forever "

They stood in the same position for some time, Andrea's arm across her shoulders and one of her arms wrapped around Andrea's waist.

"You said you received a package for me?" Cora asked, breaking the silence.

"Oh yeah... I placed it on the kitchen island," Andrea informed her.

"Okay, I'm gonna go see where it's from," Cora replied, disentangling herself from Andrea. "Are you coming?" she asked after her sister made no attempt to move.

"Go on without me," Andrea spoke up with a small smile gracing her lips. "I'll be in shortly."

Cora nodded her head in acceptance before making her way up the porch and walking through the back door.

She saw the package in question, a large manila envelope, lying on the counter with her name and current address. The return sender was the law firm handling her divorce.

Cora reached for the envelope with shaky hands and tore the top end open. She slowly removed the document she had been anticipating its arrival. When she pulled out the document, her heart slowly fell to the floor of her stomach.

It was the decree of her divorce.

She was now officially a divorced woman.

Chapter Nineteen

Cora sat at the island, fiddling with her thin platinum wedding band; the delicate diamonds around the circumference of the ring glimmered whichever way it turned as the precious stones caught the light. Why it still adorned her finger after an entire week had passed since receiving the papers, she did not know. Perhaps she was a sucker for punishment, as every time she laid eyes on the most expensive piece of jewelry she ever owned, her mind would transport her to the past. She would reflect on the happy times she'd had with Joel. But then his betrayal would rear its ugly head, and she would find herself slipping into depression.

"Cora," her mother said from behind her, "are you okay?"

Cora quickly plastered a smile on her face before turning to her mother, not wanting to upset her. Becky was already struggling with a life-threatening illness and now learning to somewhat cope without her husband. She didn't want to add her own problems to the mix.

"Yes, Mom, I'm good," she replied in what she hoped came out in a cheery enough voice. "How are you feeling?" she asked, getting up off the stool and walking toward her mother. "Is your hand okay?" Cora saw the look of sadness set on her mother's face briefly before she, too, plastered a smile on her face.

"I'm okay this morning. I wanted to come down and make breakfast for you and Andrea," her mother revealed.

"Oh," Cora replied, surprised.

"Actually, Mom, I went for a run then came back and made breakfast. Have a seat. Let me make you a plate."

Without waiting for a response, she rounded the island and started filling her mother's plate with scrambled eggs, hash browns, and a few strips of bacon. Her mother's look of disappointment had not gone unnoticed by her, but she also couldn't address it.

Cora set the plate in front of her and moved the basket with the fresh bread close enough for her to reach it. Taking a mug from the cupboard, she poured her mother some hot chocolate, then sat before her.

"So the doctor called," Cora started conversationally as she watched her mother eat.

"Oh, and?" Becky asked, not sounding the least bit interested in whatever the conversation had yielded.

"He says there's a new trial that looks promis—"

"Cora," her mother cut her off. "I told you already. I am not interested in being a part of any trials or a guinea pig. I just want to be able to live out the rest of whatever time I have left being happy and surrounded by family," she informed her daughter.

"But, Mom, this could mean the difference between you suffering and you being able to function with this disease," Cora implored, trying to get her to see reason.

Becky looked at her daughter and smiled sadly.

"You can't fix everything, Cora." Reaching over the island surface, she took her daughter's hand in her own and gently squeezed it. "I will not spend my remaining time on this earth going from trial to trial all over the country... I can't live like that, sweetie."

Cora sighed dejectedly, realizing she was arguing a moot point. Still, she could not help herself from trying one more time.

"Mom, please do it for me, for Andrea and Josephine, for your granddaughters. I can't lose you, not when I have lost so much already," she spoke intensely. She knew her bringing up her mother's loved ones and her own fears of losing her was a strategy to guilt her into doing it. The moment the words left her mouth, she regretted them. She knew it was selfish of her.

Her mother's eyes glistened with tears.

"Do you think I want to leave you all?" Her voice broke at the end as the tears burst the dam and rolled down her cheeks. "I finally have my girls back, and instead of it being the most joyful experience, it is laced with so much sadness. I am already enough of a burden to you all. I'm a burden to my own self," she cried passionately. "I can't do that to you, Cora— I can't get my hopes up like that only to be told that it doesn't work. I don't want to spend the rest of my waking moment chasing after the next best thing. That time can be spent with you girls, with my family, creating memories."

At the end of her mother's speech, Cora's eyes were just as wet as her mother's.

Moving off her seat, she went to kneel before her mother— her arms around her torso. "I'm sorry, Mom. I shouldn't have said that; I was being selfish because I don't want to lose you," she cried into her mother's stomach.

Becky ran her hand through her daughter's light-brown hair as she held her to her.

"Shh... shh, I know, sweetie," she cooed.

Cora raised her blue-gray eyes to look into her mother's eyes that looked back at her with love.

"I love you, Cora. I appreciate everything you and your

sister have been doing. You didn't have to take on the responsibility, but you did. I am honored to have a daughter like you."

Becky leaned down and kissed her daughter's forehead.

Cora's mind remained unsettled even after she, Andrea, and their mother had such a wonderful time the day before, having a mother-daughters day. They spent the day in town, sightseeing like tourists and hitting the boutiques. Andrea had made a spa appointment for them, which they went to right after their excursion. She couldn't lie. It was the best thing that she could have done. All three women had the opportunity to unwind and have the tension kneaded out of their muscles at their Swedish massage appointment. She felt refreshed and less tense, but the thoughts that seemed to occupy every waking and sleeping moment threatened to render all the work done useless. She could already feel an incessant throbbing at her temple, which she was sure would turn into a migraine if she didn't find a way to dissolve the thoughts in her mind.

"Cora, I have been looking for you."

Cora turned her head to see her sister coming toward where she sat by the rose bushes in the garden. She noticed the look of panic on her sister's face and immediately jumped up from her position.

"What is it, Andrea? Is it Mom?" she rushed out, pushing her feet into her sandals that she had abandoned as she stretched out on the garden bench.

"No, Mom's fine," Andrea hurried to say.

"What is it then? You look upset," Cora observed, rushing over to her.

"Umm... I think it is best you come and see," Andrea spoke vaguely.

This only served to raise Cora's blood pressure, and the throbbing at her temple was now thumping something fierce.

"Why can't you just tell me? Is it that bad?" she asked, panic lacing her voice.

"Well, you see... it's— it's not bad per se, but I just think it is better for you to come and see rather than I say it," Andrea reasoned.

Cora tried to protest when Andrea stopped her.

"Cora, please just trust me. It's better that you come rather than I tell you what it is," Andrea pleaded.

Begrudgingly, she nodded her head in acceptance. Andrea immediately turned and swiftly walked toward the garden's exit. Cora kept pace with her, and in less than five minutes, they were walking through the back door.

Cora followed her sister toward the living room, confused by the large suitcase and carry-on luggage by the stairs.

As soon as she stepped into the room, her confusion turned to surprise and then fear.

"Erin, what are you doing here? Is everything okay?" she asked, rushing to her eldest daughter.

As soon as she stood before her, she realized something truly was not right. There were tear stains on Erin's face, and her usually bright green eyes were dull and puffy with dark circles under them, her lips quivering as more tears threatened to run down her cheeks.

Cora's heart constricted at her daughter's appearance.

"Erin... what's wrong, sweetie?" she asked in earnest.

Instead of answering her mother, Erin threw her hands over her shoulders and sobbed uncontrollably. Cora didn't know what to do to help her daughter because she didn't know what was wrong with her. Still, she placed her hand on Erin's back and rubbed small calming circles.

"It's okay, sweetie. Whatever it is, we'll get through it together." She comforted the young woman, still sobbing into her neck.

When Erin's tears subsided, Cora ushered her toward the couch to sit down.

Andrea mouthed to Cora that she was going to check on

their mother before she exited the room, giving the two some privacy.

Cora ran her hand through Erin's brown curls attempting to calm her while she waited for her to tell her what was wrong.

"I didn't get the position at my job," Erin finally revealed as her sniffles subsided.

"Oh sweetie, I'm so sorry. I know you worked hard for that position."

Erin turned her eyes up to her mother, filled with disappointment. "Well, it didn't help me in this situation because they chose to give it to one of the execs' niece in the end," she said bitterly. "She wasn't even interning there."

Cora felt her daughter's anger at being overlooked by someone inexperienced and family. She also knew that the job world was cruel, and no matter how hard you worked, sometimes you got passed over for a less qualified person who just needed to know the right person. She had experienced a lot of that back in her days as a young journalist. However, the disappointments and the countless times she was overlooked only pushed her harder, and in the end, her hard work paid off. They couldn't ignore the fact that she was very good at what she did.

Cora reached for her daughter's shoulder and rested her hand there. "Sweetie, things like these happen all the time. It doesn't mean that you should give up. Your breakthrough will come. It might take a few more tries, but in the end, they won't be able to ignore your light," she encouraged her.

"Thanks, Mom," Erin replied gratefully, placing her hand over the one her mother had on her shoulder in appreciation.

Cora bumped her head against her daughter's lovingly.

"I believe in you, Erin. You are meant to do great things," Cora whispered against her temple. She stepped back, watching as her daughter sucked in a deep breath, collecting herself.

"So...I noticed your luggage by the stairs. Does that mean you're planning on staying here for a while?" she asked, trying to hold back a small smile.

The girl gave her a sheepish look. "Yes, I wanted to come home, but this is your home now, so I just decided to come here rather than stay back in Seattle," Erin explained. "I just need some time to clear my head and think about my next move."

Cora nodded in understanding. She was happy that Erin wanted to stay on the island, but something wasn't adding up to her. Even though she hadn't got the job back in New York, her daughter had built a life in that state for the past three years. She had friends there, an apartment that she shared with her boyfriend.

"What does Brian have to say about your decision?" she asked, watching her daughter intently.

A weird look flitted across her daughter's face at the mention of her boyfriend. Cora could not decipher what it meant.

"Brian and I decided to take some time apart." Erin dropped the news, her eyes looking anywhere but at her mother.

And there it was. Cora knew there was more to the story. She'd just hoped that was it.

Chapter Twenty

"**B**rian...I can't—" Erin sighed. "I can't give you an answer because—"

Erin pinched the bridge of her nose as she listened to whatever it was her boyfriend was saying to her.

"It's not as simple as you think," she breathed out exasperatedly. "I don't know if I'm ready to make such a big step..." Erin paused before lowering her voice barely above a whisper as she finished her sentence, "I'm still trying to figure out if this is meant to be— if we're meant to last."

Whatever Brian said to her caused Erin's eyes to glisten with unshed tears, and she folded her bottom lip between her teeth.

"I know you love me... I just... I don't know if that is enough," she spoke, putting her hand over her eyes. "I don't know when I'll be back, Brian." She paused. "I know we have to talk about this, but I can't do this right now." She sighed, resting her forehead against the pantry cabinet, eyes closed, listening to whatever it was Brian was saying.

Cora hadn't meant to eavesdrop. That was not the reason she had come downstairs. She couldn't sleep and needed a glass of water or maybe some tea. She was surprised to see the light on in the kitchen, and the soft whispering coming from there caught her off guard. As she moved closer, she realized that it was Erin on her phone. Somehow she couldn't bring herself to let her daughter, who had her back to her, know that she was there. Cora stood there by the entrance listening to the argument Erin was having with Brian.

"Fine." Erin threw her hand in the air in frustration. "Fine, Brian, I don't know if we're meant to go further because we want different things, and I don't see how we can come to a compromise..." Erin trailed off as she listened to whatever he was saying.

"I can't just say yes, just because you have a ring and—" She paused briefly before talking again. "Don't bring my dad into this, Brian. He has nothing to do with the state of our relationship. He's not the one forcing me to say yes," Erin warned as she turned around to see her mother looking straight back at her; her eyes widened in surprise.

"I'll call you back. I have to go," she rushed to say to Brian before moving the phone from her ear and ending the call.

"How... how long were you standing there?" Erin asked her mother.

The evenness of Erin's voice would have fooled Cora into thinking her daughter wasn't angry if she hadn't been paying attention to her mannerisms. Erin's arms were folded over her chest, and her right foot bounced up and down rapidly on the tiled floor.

Cora was sure her daughter already knew she had been standing there for some time, and so she went with the truth.

"I'm so sorry, sweetheart. I should have said something sooner," she apologized, moving farther into the kitchen.

"Yeah, you should have," Erin replied flippantly as she walked over to the counter and threw contents in the cup by the sink down the drain. She then turned on the faucet and began washing it.

"Erin," Cora started once more, cautiously. "I know you're upset with me for listening to your conversation with Brian, and I mean it. I am truly, truly sorry about that. I didn't even know you were in the kitchen until I stepped through the entrance, but I—"

"It's fine, Mom." Erin dismissed her apology. She still had her back to her mother even though she had finished washing the cup.

After some time of neither of them saying anything, Cora finally spoke up.

"I'm worried about you, sweetie. Why won't you talk to me?" she pleaded. Erin didn't say anything. "What's going on between you and Brian?"

"Nothing is going on with Brian, Mom." Erin whirled to look at her mother. The sharp glare made Cora take a step back.

"I just want some time to sort through my feelings, and I thought this would have been the best place to do it, but if you're going to keep questioning me every five seconds, watch my every move, and listen in on my conversations like you did a while ago then I guess this was a mistake," Erin seethed.

"Erin," Cora started, getting ready to apologize once more, but her daughter raised her hand, halting her.

"I'm tired, Mom. I just need to lie down. Can you allow me to do that?" she asked, her voice still laced with the tension that rolled off her entire body in waves.

Cora couldn't speak. Erin's outbursts had rendered her speechless. She simply nodded in agreement. Erin quickly walked past her and out of the kitchen.

Cora took a seat at the island and raised her palms to run over her face as she let out a ragged breath. She felt the guilt seep into her as she recalled how Erin's expression switched from hurt to anger when she realized her mother had been eavesdropping on her conversation with her boyfriend.

She felt the weight of what she did as Erin's words replayed in her mind. Was she that bad, pestering her daughter with questions and not realizing she needed time before she could open up to her?

She wished she could have taken back her actions from earlier but in retrospect, would she have gotten an insight into her daughter's current situation? Like the fact that it seemed Brian wanted to take the next step in their relationship, but Erin was looking to pump the brakes, possibly ending it altogether.

Her mind went back to one of the last things she heard before the call ended. She knew that Erin was still hurt by what her father had done— she still hadn't spoken to him in the past several months, and probably it was having an adverse effect on her relationship with her boyfriend.

Cora knew Erin had loved her father so much that she idolized him. He had been the kind of father that any girl would have wanted. He was supportive of both his daughters, making every effort to be at all of their school events. He had family time with them; he took them to their sleepovers, stood protectively by their sides, grilling their dates and reminding them that he would do anything for his princesses. Erin had spoken about it openly that she wanted to find someone like her father, to love her as he loved Cora and his family.

He had never done anything to disappoint Erin, not until he cheated on Cora.

Cora's heart constricted at the knowledge that Joel's betrayal had affected her girls more than they had been willing to share. Now she didn't know when Erin would be willing to open up to her again. In times like these, she wished her skills in journalism would work on her daughter.

Sighing, she got up from the stool, and went and poured herself a glass of water. She gulped it down and returned to her room to continue to toss and turn as she willed sleep to come.

When Cora made it downstairs again, it was too early for anyone to be up. She had decided to go for a run instead. She was surprised to see her daughter at the bottom of the stairs in full running gear.

At her descent, Erin looked at the stairs and up at her before looking at the floor.

"Good morning," Cora said softly to her daughter.

"Good morning. I wanted to go for a run, but I realized I didn't know the area that well, so I decided to wait here for you because I guessed that you still maintained your early morning run," Erin explained. "Looks like I guessed right." She gave her mom a brief smile.

Cora returned her daughter's small, genuine smile. She saw it as a sign that Erin wasn't entirely mad at her and was glad. Any opportunity that she got to spend with her daughter was a blessing, seeing that her interests and advice in their lives were no longer eagerly solicited.

"Of course, honey," she readily agreed. "I know this place like the back of my hand. Even after being away for so long and the many changes I've seen, I know all the main roads, sites, and the parks good for running."

Erin looked at her with a small smile.

"Okay, lead the way... you're the expert." She gestured with her hands toward the front door for her mother to go before her.

Cora kept pace with her daughter as they ran along the dirt path by the highway. It was exhilarating to feel the clean, fresh air enter her lungs as her limbs burned from the exertion of moving her body forward. The dark sky had brightened to a light blue shade with striations of pink overlaid by an orange tint. Very soon, the sun would be making its appearance over the horizon, bathing the sky in its brilliant orange rays.

Cora looked over at her daughter and noticed how relaxed she looked as her eyes looked up at the sky, and a small smile rested on her lips. She wondered what was going through her mind at this very moment.

"Whew, that was great," Erin breathed out as she put her hands on her knees and tried to catch her breath.

"I just can't get over how beautiful this place is," she gushed.

Cora smiled at her daughter knowingly. "I want to show you something," she invited, turning toward the back of the house.

Erin followed her until they passed the forested area that opened up to the harbor before them.

"Oh wow, this is..." Erin was rendered speechless by the view before her.

"I know," Cora spoke in agreement.

What could be more beautiful than mountains that touched and blended so perfectly with both the light blue and white of the sky and the deep turquoise of the ocean?

"It truly is beautiful, Mom," Erin gushed.

Cora nodded in agreement.

"I wanted to show you something else." She took her daughter's hand and led her to the dock where the boat featured predominantly under its upper deck.

"Oh, does this boat belong to us?"

"Yes." Cora laughed at her daughter's excitement. "It was Dad's; he left it to me, Andrea, and Josephine," she informed her.

"I know how much you love the water, so I thought maybe we could have a day out on the ocean... only if you want to."

156

Erin walked over to her mother and put her hands over her shoulders, hugging her. Cora's hands remained at her side from the shock of her daughter so readily hugging her after last night's blow-up.

"I'm sorry for going off on you last night, Mom," she apologized.

At the anguish in her daughter's voice, Cora's hand immediately went up to hug her back.

"It's okay, sweetie. I shouldn't have eavesdropped on your conversation," she soothed her.

Erin lifted her head to look at her mother with moisture in her eyes. She gave her a grateful smile before letting her go.

Erin turned away from her. She folded her arms around her and looked out over the harbor.

Cora watched her, pained by her obvious distress.

"Brian asked me to marry him," she revealed with a soft sigh. "I told him no, and then I jumped on the first plane back to Seattle and then came here."

Cora smiled sadly at her daughter. She had surmised as much.

"I told him I just need time to figure some stuff out, but he won't stop calling," she breathed out, her shoulders sagging at the end.

"When you say *stuff*, what do you mean?" Cora asked, praying she had not pushed too hard too soon after her daughter decided to open up to her.

Erin sighed again. "Like, I don't know if I want to live in New York anymore, or if I want to work in an advertising firm," she listed. After a pause, she continued, "Or if I made a mistake settling down so soon."

Cora heard the regret in her voice and her heart broke for her. Those were some serious questions. Going over to her daughter, she placed her hands around her waist from behind, resting her chin on her shoulder. "You're strong, sweetie. I know that whatever decision you make, you'll be okay. You know why?"

"Why?" Erin asked, turning her head to look at her mother from the corner of her eye.

"Because you're my daughter, and I'll support whatever decision you make," Cora promised.

Chapter Twenty-One

Three weeks had flown by, and the smell of summer was fast approaching.

"Mom?" Cora called as she knocked on Becky's door. No answer came.

"Mom, are you okay?" she called again. She tried the knob, but the door was closed.

"I'm fine, Cor-a." She heard her mother say behind the closed door.

"Are you sure? Do you need any help?" she asked, concerned.

The door swung open to reveal Becky's irritated face.

"I...s-a-i-d I'm f-i-ne, can you j j-ust give me some privacy pl-ease?" she slurred.

"Oh, I'm sorry, Mom... it's just you didn't come down for breakfast, and it's now past eleven," Cora tried to explain.

Becky raised her left hand, stopping Cora from continuing. Cora watched as her hand lowered to her side.

Becky sighed. "I'll be down s-o-o-n."

Cora struggled to keep the sadness she felt at bay as she

watched her mother struggle to speak. It was so upsetting to see how fast the disease was progressing. Her right hand seemed to only work when it wanted to, and her left hand was gradually following. Her speech was now starting to show signs of the disease as well. Some days were good, but others were worse.

The doctor explained that the nerve cells found in the lower parts of the brain were deteriorating; hence, the muscles that move the lips, tongue, soft palate, jaw, and vocal folds were impacted; hence, speech would become difficult as time went on.

Cora and Andrea took turns helping her to get ready in the mornings when she was having difficulty.

Uncle Luke and Aunt Maria had shown up last evening to take her out just to get her mind off what was happening to her, but she locked herself away in her room, refusing to go out in public.

Cora and Andrea were at their wit's end about what to do. She didn't want to be enrolled in the trials. It felt as if she was giving up.

Thinking back to Kathleen's advice from a while back, it didn't seem like such a bad idea to get her counseling. Maybe that could help her cope better with what was happening to her.

"Okay, I'll heat some food for you," Cora said, giving her an encouraging smile. She left her mother and headed for the kitchen to put her mother's plate in the microwave.

"How's Mom?" Andrea asked as she and Erin entered the kitchen and took seats by the island.

"Umm, she's..." Cora didn't know how to finish the sentence, so she shrugged helplessly, "I don't know. Where are you guys coming from?" she asked, changing the topic.

"Auntie Andrea took me whale watching." Erin grinned.

Cora chuckled at her daughter's child-like wonder. It was

like a window to the past when her daughter was a child. Those had been simpler times.

Andrea smiled back at her niece before turning to Cora, expression somber. "I'm gonna check on Mom," she informed her.

Cora nodded in acknowledgment.

As soon as Andrea exited the room, she turned her attention to her daughter. "Sounds like you had a lot of fun."

"It was great. I mean, I almost lost my head at how big and terrifying those things looked, but after I got used to it, I got to admire it all," she explained.

"I'm glad," Cora told her, turning to the microwave to remove the plate and pull off the wrap. Cora got a tray to put the dish on, deciding if their mother still didn't come downstairs, she would have to take the meal up to her. She hadn't eaten much since yesterday, so she must be hungry.

"Hi, Grandma, how are you feeling?" Cora heard her daughter ask.

She turned to see her mother enter the kitchen, her left hand resting on Erin's shoulder.

"I'm fine, sweetheart." Her mother smiled reassuringly at Erin. It warmed Cora's heart.

Even though Becky had barely spoken to her or Andrea in the past week, she didn't seem to have a problem talking with Erin.

"Mom," Cora spoke, catching her mother's attention, "do you want to eat here or out on the patio?"

"I'll eat here,'" Becky informed her.

Cora nodded before setting the plate before her. "I'm going to talk to Andrea real quick," she informed them. "Is she still upstairs?" she directed to her mother.

"No, sh-she went outside," Becky replied.

"Okay, thanks, Mom." Cora left out through the back door in search of her sister.

She found her out by the swing, casually kicking her legs as she swung back and forth.

"Hey," Cora greeted her sister as soon as she was standing directly behind her.

Andrea looked over at her sister as the swing brought her up and forward.

"Hey yourself," she greeted, bringing the swing to a stop.

"I think Mom should go to counseling. I think any type of therapy at this point would be a huge help," Cora told her sister as she moved to her side. "I think it will give her the right coping skills to deal with what she's feeling— the rapidness of changes is taking a toll on her mentally. I know it is taking a toll on me because I don't know what to do." Cora sighed.

"I agree with you," Andrea consented. "The hard part is getting her to see the need to do it."

"Yeah, that's going to be a difficult conversation." Cora chuckled unhappily. "Maybe if we did it like an intervention, that could get her to see the need for it," she offered as a solution.

"Yeah, maybe." Andrea's voice was laced with uncertainty.

The two sisters stood under the old oak, looking out over the property, contemplative as they tried to figure out a way to get their mother to talk to someone.

"Oh, before I forget, Jo called. She says she has a couple more loose ends to tie up, but she's hoping to be here by the end of the month," Andrea informed her.

"That's great news," Cora replied. "Is she sure she wants to do this, though? I mean, she had a promising career and all," Cora wondered in concern.

"She's sure." Andrea tucked a strand of hair behind her ear. "I think she needs the change in scenery, you know? To be somewhere where she can be surrounded by people who care for her— her family. People who she knows will have her back no matter what."

Cora nodded in agreement.

"She's hurting bad, isn't she?" she asked.

Josephine had called her more times in the past few months than she had in any given year for over twenty years. Even though their relationship had gotten better, and they talked and laughed about when they were kids and happier times, she knew that the gapped years still had an invisible grip on their relationship, preventing it from becoming more than just reminiscing about the past and bonding over the loss they experienced as sisters. She wanted the opportunity to be a support for her now, considering she hadn't since the day she left Oak Harbor all those years ago.

"Yeah," Andrea admitted. "She's not getting more than four hours of sleep every day, and things about the accident fill her with so much pain and regret."

Cora's heart tightened at the revelation. She wanted to be there for her sister like she never had the opportunity to be before.

"I'm glad she has you to talk to," she stared at Andrea with gratitude.

"Yeah." Andrea sighed. "Only, she doesn't let me that far in. I think there is more going on that she's not saying," she revealed.

"Like what?" Cora asked.

"I don't really know. I just have this nagging feeling that she's holding back something important."

"Well, then it's a good thing she's coming home. Maybe being here, being around us, will make her comfortable enough to open up."

"Yeah, I hope you're right." Andrea looked at her from the corner of her eyes.

Cora hoped so too.

"Have you figured out a way to deal with your own predicament?" she asked, looking straight at Andrea.

Andrea ran her hand through her hair as her lips cast down in a frown. Sighing, she turned to her sister to reveal the look of trepidation in her blue eyes.

Cora reached out and touched her arm comfortingly.

"I called her and told her I need to speak with her," Andrea confessed. "But now I feel like I made a huge mistake." She sighed.

"You're strong, Andrea," Cora encouraged her sister, bringing her closer to her side and placing her hand over her shoulder for a side hug.

"You can do this, and Aurora will understand."

Andrea rested her head against her sister's. "Thank you, Cora. I don't know what I would do if I didn't have you here. I'm happy we found each other again," she expressed gratefully.

"I'm glad we did," Cora agreed. Reaching over with her free hand, she wiped the lone tear that had escaped her sister's glistening eyes. "I promise from now on that I will always be there for you, little sis," she spoke with feeling.

Andrea gave her a wide, grateful smile.

"So... how do we get Mom to agree to get counseling?" she asked, pulling away from Cora and kneading her eyes with the palms of her hands.

"I don't know, but I think we should do it as soon as possible."

Andrea nodded in agreement.

"Why don't we do it today?" she offered.

"I thought we should do it when she's in a better mood, actually," Cora shared.

Andrea looked at her sister with a raised brow. "Cora," she said seriously. "Judging by what we've seen so far, when do you actually think Mom will ever be in a better mood again?"

Cora thought through her sister's words carefully.

"You're right. We should do it now," she acquiesced.

The two of them headed for the house, hoping that they would be able to convince their mother to speak with someone.

When they got inside, they were surprised to see that their mother was no longer in the kitchen.

"Hey, Mom. Are you looking for Grandma?" Cora heard Erin ask from behind her.

"Oh, yes, sweetie. Do you know where she went?"

Erin nodded her head before pointing up the stairs. "Grandma said she needed to lie down for a bit, so she went back to her room."

"Thanks, sweetie." Cora gave her daughter a grateful smile before she and Andrea made their way upstairs.

"Mom?" she called, knocking on the door lightly.

"What is it, Cora?" her mother called from inside the room.

"Can we come in? Andrea and I— there's something we need to discuss," she called out for her mother to hear.

After a minute, the door swung open, and their mother stood before them, looking exhausted and gloomy.

"What is it?" she asked tiredly.

Cora sighed inwardly, saddened to see her mother so dejected. She had lost some weight in the past two months since Cora had been there. The blue dress she had on used to fit her body nicely, but now it hung off her frame, making her look fragile.

"Can we come in?" she asked, to which Becky moved aside to let them walk into the room.

After settling down, they turned to their mother, determination written on their faces.

"Mom," Cora began softly, "I know it's difficult for you to deal with this illness, and we wish there were more we could do to make it easier for you."

"We don't want you to feel any less than or that you're a burden because you're not," Andrea jumped in. "We're just happy to have you in our lives again. We want you to know that."

Becky looked at her daughters with an unreadable expression, making Cora nervous about what could possibly be going on in her head.

"Mom, we love you. We only want the best for you, and we want to spend this time with you, making sure you're happy," Cora continued.

Reaching over, she clasped her mother's hands in her own and massaged her fingers before she continued.

"Mom, Andrea and I were talking, and we think it is necessary that you talk to someone—maybe a professional, like a counselor in order to deal with everything that's going on. What do you think?"

Cora could see the defeat in her mother's eyes, and a lump formed in her throat as her mother nodded in response. She knew this was going to be a long hard road. Cora was just grateful that her mother agreed.

Chapter Twenty-Two

Cora looked out at the astounding stretch of the blue-green water glistening as the overhead sun cast its bright rays across its surface, the undulating white-capped waves breaking the uniformity of it all. The mountains on the horizon had long discarded their snowy caps as they reflected the change in seasons. No matter how many times Cora found herself by the harbor, she would never tire of marveling at the beautiful scenery she was blessed to have right in her very own backyard.

She was able to do some of her best thinking and reflecting on all that had been happening in her life— here and after having a good run.

She thought about all that had happened in the past nine months. She was now a divorced forty-five-year-old woman with two grown children, each with their own sets of problems. Her father had passed away and left the business to her and her sisters, and her mother was battling a neurological disease that was rapidly shutting down her body's ability to carry out the functions it was created for and would ultimately kill her. It was a lot to deal with.

She fiddled with the ring still positioned on her wedding finger. She had thought to remove it on countless occasions but had chickened out at the last minute every time. Somehow in her mind, this piece of metal was the only thing that represented some semblance of normalcy in her life. It was what she had worn for the past twenty-three years. It had been through it all with her. She couldn't find the heart to part with it.

"Hey," she heard the masculine voice say from behind her. Looking over her shoulder, she saw him standing there looking at her with a smile gracing his lips.

Cora turned fully to face him, a small smile gracing her own lips.

"Hi," she spoke softly and took a breath before continuing. "When did you get back?" she asked, cursing the way her voice sounded so breathy.

"Just yesterday," he informed her.

"I'm glad you made it back safe." Cora cringed at the way her words sounded in her ears.

He chuckled as his dark eyes glinted with mirth. "I'm glad to be back too, safe," he spoke softly.

She smiled again, all of a sudden feeling shy. "So how was LA?" she asked, moving the conversation into safer waters.

"LA was great. I didn't get to see much because the project took up most of my waking hours," he explained. "I won't lie, though; they have some great architecture back out that side," he spoke with appreciation.

Cora smiled at his passion. He had been gone for the past two weeks, which had put their budding friendship on hold. A friend had contacted him to come to help him finish a huge project in LA because he was behind. He had taken the offer, promising that he'd be back before the month ended. The projects he had in Oak Harbor had been in their finishing stages, so he had left his workmen in charge of finishing up. Even Kathleen's house was almost finished renovating. It was possible that before the end of the week, it would be finished.

"I was actually on my way somewhere, but I wanted to stop and say hi," he spoke up, rubbing the back of his neck. "I guess what I wanted to say is... I missed you. What I mean is that I missed my friend."

The awkward way the words fell out of his mouth as he tried to explain himself warmed Cora's heart, and she couldn't stop the wide grin that spread across her face. His face appeared slightly flushed like that of a teenage boy.

"Anyway, I gotta go," he said, turning away from her, seemingly embarrassed by the situation.

"Okay," Cora returned, not wanting to make him feel any more awkward than he probably was already feeling. But then she called out, "Wait, where are you going?"

Jamie turned to her, his eyes taking on a haunting sadness that confused Cora.

"I'm going to go visit my mother's grave. Today would have been her birthday," he told her.

She had suspected as much that his mother was no longer alive based on the last conversation they had about her but hearing him confirm it and the sadness he undoubtedly still had from her passing tugged at Cora's heart.

Cora found herself walking toward him, and as soon as she was standing before him, she placed her hands around his torso and hugged him, hoping he felt the comfort she was trying to give him from such a simple gesture.

Jamie's hands remained at his side for some time as if he was surprised that she was actually hugging him, but then they came up to hold her to his body.

"I'm sorry for your loss," she whispered against his chest.

He didn't say anything, and for a while, the two just held

on to each other, neither offering another word but rather drawing strength from the other.

"To this day, it hurts to know that she died so young," he spoke, the regret evident in his voice.

Cora moved back from hugging him to look up into his eyes.

"I could come with you.... If you want," she offered.

Jamie looked at her, his expression unreadable.

"I mean, I don't want to impose, but I just want to be able to help you in any way I can because I now know what this grief is like," she rushed to say.

His face broke out into a warm smile that caused the sides of his eyes to crinkle.

"You're an amazing person, do you know that?"

Cora blinked, surprised by his revelation.

"I would very much appreciate it if you would accompany me," he expressed.

Cora sat in the car listening to Jamie's recount of his childhood. His mother had been a single mother after his father, who was an army man, was killed overseas in a raid gone wrong when he was just three. She had done her best to make sure that he had everything he needed. She had supported all of his dreams, and when it came time for him to go to college to become an architect, she surprised him with the death gratuity money she had received from her husband's death.

"But then she got the news that she had Parkinson's Disease and because I was in my final year of college, she kept the news from me." He sighed.

"I didn't find out until she was too sick to help herself. I left everything back in New York and moved home to take care of her. That's how I met Brooke," he continued to say.

Cora's interest in the story peaked even more at the mention of his deceased wife.

"She was a nurse at the hospital. I had to take Mom for her

injections. She was in the room helping Mom one of the days I was with her. I walked into the room, and there she was, explaining to Mom how she would be administering the shot. She looked up at me with those pretty hazel eyes, and when she smiled, I knew my life wouldn't be the same if I didn't have her in mine," he spoke with fondness.

Cora looked over at him and noticed the faraway look that marred his face when he spoke about his wife. She smiled sadly, wishing she was able to make his painless.

"I wouldn't trade the time I got to spend with either of them for anything, but I've realized that even though I will always have them in my memory, sometimes when I think about them, it'll make me sad. I have to keep moving forward. I have to open myself up to making new memories, finding new friendships, and new love."

At the latter part of his statement, Cora's heart skipped a beat as telltale flutters were felt in her stomach.

She looked through the window of her side of the truck, watching the scenes go by as she waited for the warmness she felt in her chest and face to subside.

They remained in comfortable silence for the past fifteen minutes of the drive, each lost in their own thoughts. Soon the truck was pulling past the sign, **Welcome to Langley Lawn Cemetery**. Jamie parked at the designated parking area and came around to Cora's side to open the door for her. Her heart warmed at his act of chivalry, and her heart rate sped up the moment their hands touched as he assisted her from the seat. She nearly lost her balance as her foot slipped off the side step, but he deftly caught her by the waist, bringing her down to the ground, directly in front of him. As if drawn by some invisible force, her blue-gray eyes lifted to his obsidian ones that looked straight back at her. Her heart started to beat erratically against her chest and what little air she had left in her lungs seemingly was only enough to keep her from fainting.

One hand still held her waist possessively as the other rose toward her face.

A car pulling up beside the truck snapped them out of whatever trance they had found themselves in, and Cora quickly stepped away from him.

Jamie's hand dropped to his side while his eyes reflected what she was sure was a disappointment, but as quickly as it had registered, it had disappeared. He smiled charmingly at her as he moved past her to close the truck door. "Ready to go?" he asked, still sporting the smile.

"After you." Cora gestured before her for him to lead the way.

"Wait, let me just get a few things," he said, going to the back door and pulling out a bouquet of yellow daisies, a bottle of wine, and two wine flutes.

"These were her favorite," he said, holding up the bright-colored flowers.

Cora admired the effort he made to honor his mother even though she was no longer here. She was sure he must have been a very loving son when his mom was alive.

"Do you do this often? Take flowers, I mean?" she asked.

"On special occasions like her birthday and the anniversary of her death," he explained.

Cora nodded in understanding.

"Ready to go?" he asked, turning toward what she perceived was the direction of his mother's tombstone. She quickly stepped to his side, and they took off down the concrete path laid in the middle of the low bright green expanse of the lawn interrupted by tombstones of the dead buried under their grassy surface at intervals.

They came to a stop at a tombstone marked with the name "Luanne Theresa Hillier." A vase with wilted yellow daisies was positioned above the writing. Jamie reached down and took up the vase. Removing the dead flowers, he then placed fresh water in the container and added a new vibrant bouquet of yellow and pink carnations that he had brought with him. He stooped down to wipe off the headstone before placing the vase back in the position it was in. Cora stood above him, watching and feeling as if she was intruding on an intimate moment.

"Hi, Mom," Jamie started softly. "I brought you some fresh flowers for your birthday... Happy Birthday, Mom."

Cora didn't know what else to do but standby and allow him to have this time with his mother and possibly offer support where it was needed.

"I brought someone for you to meet— a friend. Her name is Cora. She reminds me so much of you and your caring nature. She has a tendency to put everyone's needs above her own, but she's also very smart and funny— even though she doesn't know it and a great listener. I think you two would have been great friends."

At Jamie's indirect complements, Cora's face grew warm, and she was sure the evidence was also on her cheeks.

The two spent the next hour drinking the wine in celebration of his mother while he chose to tell a few more stories about his childhood and the antics he carried out that landed him in the hot seat with her on countless occasions.

Cora hadn't laughed this much in a long time. The more elaborate the stories he recounted, the more relaxed she became, laughing at his unfortunate encounters and even teasing him a few times.

Cora looked down into the wineglass, still half filled with the sweet wine. She frowned as she thought about her own mother's illness and how little they were able to help her other than just being there for her.

"Penny for your thoughts?"

Cora looked up to see Jamie watching her carefully, awaiting her answer to his question.

Cora sighed in defeat as she gave him a soft smile filled with all the sadness she felt.

"Mom is dying." She exhaled. "And there is nothing we can do to reverse it."

Jamie gave her an understanding look that encouraged her to continue. "She has ALS, and in the past two weeks, she has lost about sixty percent functionality in her right hand, and her left hand is gradually joining the list. Her speech has slowed, and some days are worse than others. She refuses to leave the house, not wanting anyone to see her. Andrea and I suggested counseling, and after much convincing, she decided to give it a try." She sighed again as her shoulders drooped in defeat. "More times than not, I feel like I'm out of my element, and I just wish there was a manual to follow to operate on autopilot."

Jamie gave her a sympathetic look. "Want my advice?" he asked. Without waiting for an answer, he continued, "Take some time for yourself— to work on your mental health and wellness; otherwise, you'll be too burnt out to help anyone, including your mom. I'm only saying this because I've been there. I was so worried about my mom that one evening while coming from the hospital in the latter stages of her illness, my mind was so consumed with hurt and confusion that I almost ran off the road," he spoke, shaking his head at the memory. "From that moment, I decided that in order to take care of my mom and those I loved, I had to take care of me too." He focused his eyes back on her.

"Don't let that happen to you, Cora," he implored.

She nodded in agreement.

"I've been meaning to tell you that you deserve so much more than you are willing to accept right now but don't cut yourself off from experiencing new things. It might just be the very thing you need to open the door for the extraordinary thing you have been waiting for."

Chapter Twenty-Three

I t had been a week since Jamie took Cora to his mother's grave, and in that short space of time, she had revealed so much about her personal life than she had with anyone except her sisters. It felt freeing to be able to talk to someone who understood where she was coming from— where her headspace was, and Jamie did very well in that area. She was grateful for their friendship and the way it had progressed. But then there were times she felt as if she was getting too attached; as if the first thing she would want to do as soon as she woke in the mornings was to call him and for his voice to be the last one she heard before heading off to sleep.

"You're doing it again," he said to her four days into their official friendship when she tried to avoid him, giving him excuses about how busy she was.

"You're in your head again," he had said to her, putting his hands on her shoulders and staring intently into her eyes. It had

been a mistake to let him touch her because it only caused the constant warmness that she felt when she was around him to become a raging fire. She got lost in his onyx eyes and had to shake her head to clear the fog and focus on his words.

"In order for this friendship to work, we have to communicate," he continued to say. "Now, yesterday when you ignored my calls and my texts really hurt my feelings." He pouted, pushing out his lips and giving her puppy eyes.

Cora couldn't help the unearthly sound that left her lips at his antics. She hurriedly clasped her hand over her mouth as she looked at him with wide, horrified eyes.

"That was so cute." He laughed.

"It was not," she cried indignantly, after which she burst into laughter, joining him.

"You're so crazy," she said, shaking her head.

Jamie smirked, and once again, her heart rate spiked.

"Will you pick up my calls and read my texts from now on?" he asked.

She nodded in agreement. "Good." He smiled widely before walking off in the direction of the inn.

"Hi, Cora."

Cora looked over her shoulder to see Kathleen coming toward her as she stood talking to Marg by the receptionist's desk as she provided her with an update on the guests who were currently at the inn.

"Hi, Kathleen. How are you?" she asked. "How are the renovations coming along?"

"I'm fine, thanks. The renovations will be finished this weekend. I actually wanted to speak to you about that," she continued.

"Oh, okay. I'll catch up with you later, Marg," Cora said to the woman behind the desk, who gave her a bright knowing smile.

"Actually, this involves Marg as well."

Cora drew her brow in confusion.

"I was thinking of having a housewarming get-together this Monday as the house will be finished. This is your official invite," she spoke, waiting expectantly for their response.

"I would be delighted to attend," Cora consented, flashing her a knowing smile.

"Count me in," Marg chimed in.

"Wonderful!" Kathleen exclaimed gratefully. "I'm on my way to the mall to get a few things to help with the décor," she explained. She took off for the entrance but halted and turned toward them once more. "Before I forget, I wanted to say thank you for making me feel welcome here. I am truly grateful. Also, I was offered the position of head of psychology at Whidbey Public Hospital," she expressed, a very pleased smile sketched on her face.

Cora blinked back her surprise. "Wow, that's great news. Are you planning on staying in Whidbey then?" she asked cautiously, hoping it wouldn't cause offense by asking.

Kathleen looked on contemplatively for a while, making Cora regret having asked the question.

"I'm not sure yet," she finally answered. "I still had five months until my leave is up. I explained it to the medical director, but 'try it out' were his words, and perhaps it'll give me a reason to want to stay and become a part of the hospital permanently."

"Okay, I understand," Cora expressed.

"I'll see you all later," Kathleen spoke as she turned on her way out the door.

"Hmm, what do you make of that?" Cora turned to her receptionist to ask.

Marg smiled. "What I think is that the island is working its magic on poor Ms. Kathleen. I'm betting at the end of her time here, she won't have the heart to leave anymore," she predicted, eyes twinkling knowingly.

"Poor Kathleen." Cora repeated the woman's words sympathetically before bursting into laughter. "You're right, Marg. This island does seem to have some magical hold on the people who come here," she mused. Marg nodded in agreement.

Just then, a young man who looked to be in his twenties walked through the door. His honey blond hair was caught in a messy man bun at the back of his head, and he sported a light beard that was shaped probably by his barber to fit his angular face, running from the sides to under his neck. He stood in the hall, looking around as if assessing the place. Finally, he set his eyes on the two women at the desk to the side watching him.

Instant recognition flashed in Cora's blue-gray eyes as she looked back at her daughter's boyfriend staring back at her, recognition evident in his cerulean blue eyes flecked with gold around the pupils.

"Brian?" Cora's voice shook with the shock she felt at his presence.

"Hi, Mrs. Avlon," the young man spoke, smiling sheepishly at her.

Cora smiled back at him as she went over and held him in her arms. She hadn't seen him in over a year and a half, and she supposed that's why she hadn't recognized him instantly as he had gone through so many changes since the last time she saw him.

"It's so good to see you," she spoke, holding him at arms-length to inspect him. He seemed taller, more muscular, but then again, she hadn't seen him in a long time.

"You look good," she spoke genuinely, looking up into the face of the six-foot-three young man.

Brian blushed at her compliment. "Thank you, Mrs. Avl—"

"Please just call me Cora or Ms. Cora if you wish," she interrupted him.

He gave her an apologetic smile.

"So I'm guessing you're here to see Erin," Cora stated the obvious.

"Umm, yeah," Brian replied, awkwardly rubbing his hand right along the leg of his dark jeans. "I haven't seen her yet, but I hope to do so once I have settled in," he stated.

It was then that Cora looked behind him to see the large suitcase by the door. Cora gave him a sympathetic smile. Her heart went out to the young man before her. She had no doubt that he loved her daughter very much, but she was also aware that even though her daughter loved him too, it might not be enough to save their relationship.

"So, what is your strategy?" Cora asked, genuinely interested in what he planned.

"Well, I don't really have a plan per se," he spoke timidly. "I just wanted to see her, to talk with her," he explained. "That's all I have so far."

Cora gave him another sympathetic smile.

"That might not be enough, Brian," she told him truthfully. "You need a plan of action that involves reminding Erin why she fell in love with you in the first place," she advised.

Brian looked away from Cora guiltily, probably kicking himself mentally for not having thought far enough ahead.

"Why don't we get you settled first, and then you can think about your plan of action?" Cora said, gesturing to the luggage behind him.

She made her way over to the house after helping Marg tidy up the room that Brian would be staying in. On the ten-minute walk, she thought about her daughter's state of mind. Would she be able to handle seeing Brian now that she was just settling into a routine? At any rate, she knew that the two needed to talk, to clear the air and decide where they went from here.

She had advised her daughter that whatever decision she made, she would support her. If Brian, therefore, blew this one chance he had, there was no way for her to help him.

"Hi, sweetie," Cora greeted, giving her daughter a light kiss on the top of her head before sitting beside her on the sofa in the den.

"Hey, Mom," she returned. "Aunt Andrea took Grandma to her counseling appointment, and she asked me to remind you to pick up Aunt Jo from the ferry terminal."

"Got it. Thanks, sweetie."

Erin smiled at her mother before turning her attention back to the television. The two sat in silence as Cora became engrossed in the documentary her daughter was watching.

"I'm gonna get ready to pick up your aunt," Cora informed her daughter, getting up from the couch. She still had an hour to go before Josephine arrived, but with the knowledge that Brian should be stopping by shortly, she thought it best to make herself disappear to give them privacy to talk. As soon as Cora made it downstairs, there was a knock on the door, but Erin was already positioned there.

"Brian?" She heard her daughter breathe out in disbelief as her boyfriend stood before her at the door.

"Hi, Erin," he greeted with a small smile. Erin stood at the door unmoving, still unable to process the fact that her boyfriend stood before her.

"These are for you," he said, handing her a bouquet of white, long-stemmed roses and a large white teddy bear. Erin's arms worked mechanically to take the gifts he offered.

"I'll leave you two to talk," Cora murmured, making her way through the front door.

* * *

180

"Hi, Jo," Cora greeted her sister with a genuine smile.

"Hi, Cora," she replied, coming up to her and wrapping her arms around her. This caught Cora by surprise, but she immediately returned the sentiment to her sister, happy for the contact.

"Let me help you with your bags," she offered as soon as the two separated.

"Thanks, Cora." Josephine smiled gratefully.

She took the suitcase and one of the shoulder bags from her sister and trudged over to her SUV to place them in the back. Soon they were on the road heading home.

"A few more of my things should be arriving next week," she informed Cora. She nodded her understanding.

"How's Tracy?" Cora asked.

"She's doing okay," Josephine replied. "I think she's happy that I will be staying here for a while," Josephine revealed.

"I'm happy you'll be here too," Cora spoke, looking over at her sister.

Josephine turned her head, giving her sister a warm smile.

"Cora," she heard her sister say hesitantly. "Something has been eating away at me for a few months now, and I don't know what to do with this knowledge. It's so burdensome."

At the heavy tiredness in her sister's voice, Cora pulled the car over. "What is it, Jo? You can tell me— I know I haven't been there for you in the past, and I can't take it back, but I can be here for you now. I made a vow never to allow any of you to go through the pain and grief by yourselves ever again," she promised.

Josephine gave her a teary-eyed smile. "It's terrible, Cora," she sobbed.

Cora pulled her sister to her, allowing her to let out the sorrow and confusion she felt.

After Josephine's tears had subsided, Cora brought her face away from her shoulder to look at her tenderly.

"Why don't you start at the beginning? I have all the time to listen," she offered supportively.

Chapter Twenty-Four

Another month had passed since Josephine came home to Oak Harbor. Cora couldn't be happier, especially seeing how much it had had a positive impact on their mother's depression— that along with her therapy sessions. Becky was more talkative with her daughters, and she gave them permission to be more involved in her care, and they were all learning the true meaning of being patient.

Their bond had strengthened even more as they not just bonded over their desire to care for their mother but also the secrets they had shared among themselves. Cora was overjoyed by the fact that her two sisters had so much trust in her to share their darkest secrets with her, and she was happy to be a comforting shoulder for them to cry on and someone they considered to have enough wisdom to offer advice in their distress.

Erin was still in Oak Harbor. She and Brian were still on a break, but he had come to understand that she needed this time to find herself. Even though he had left Oak Harbor broken-hearted, out of the love he had for her, he had accepted her decision, reminding her he would wait for her, and even if she chose never to come back, she would always be in his heart. It was the sweetest thing Cora had ever witnessed, and it made her sad for him, but she also realized that her daughter needed the time for her mental well-being.

Her youngest daughter, Julia, was overseas on a work and travel program. Even though Cora was worried about her being all the way across the other side of the ocean in Europe, she knew she had to give her the space to continue living her life. None of her babies were truly babies anymore.

"Earth to Cora." The hand waving before her brought her out of her reverie, and at the face before her, she couldn't help the wide smile that broke out on her face.

"Well, hello there, friend," she said teasingly to the man standing before her as she remained stationary on the swing.

Jamie gave her a lopsided grin as he held the rope and gently pulled her forward before releasing it so that she could sway back and forth before him. Cora smiled up at him, enjoying his company

Their friendship had been one of the things that she was most appreciative of. She hadn't realized how much she had needed someone, not until she had no other choice but to accept his invitation to be her friend.

While her stomach still fluttered with butterflies and her heart often beat erratically at his closeness, what she cherished most was the time he spent listening to her talk about the things in her life—her wants, her fears, her disappointments—and never once making her feel as if her thoughts weren't valid. He always could tell when she was feeling down or just over-whelmed, and he always knew just how to cheer her up.

She really liked him for that, and perhaps the emotion she was feeling was a little stronger than that, but she wasn't ready to look too deeply into that.

Jamie continued to watch her swing back and forth before

him. She found herself lost in the depths of his intense stare, and every time the swing pulled away from him, she wanted it to come back immediately so that she could be closer to his line of sight.

Cora brought her feet down to steady the swing and bring it to a halt. Jamie continued to stare intently, and she felt her heartbeat pick up speed as her palms became slightly damp.

"I like you, Cora," he spoke without warning, catching her off guard. She inhaled sharply as her heart threatened to take flight if it beat any faster than it was now.

"I mean, I like you a lot. I've never felt this drawn to anyone. Not since my late wife," he confessed seriously.

When Cora didn't say anything but stare at him wide-eyed, he continued.

"It scares me how much I've gotten attached to you in such a short time, but I'm also not willing to back away from it. I feel like this deserves a shot."

Cora waited anxiously for him to continue, anticipating what he would say next.

Jamie ran his hand over the back of his neck nervously and seemingly unsure of how to continue with the conversation.

"Umm, what I'm saying is..." He swallowed and looked away from her. Cora's hands felt as if someone had spilled water on them.

Finally, he focused on her once more, determination in his eyes.

"What I'm saying, Cora, is that I enjoy your company very much. My feelings for you have grown from us just having a platonic relationship, and I think you feel the same way too. If that is the case, then I would like to take you on an official date this Saturday."

Cora couldn't get her mouth to cooperate. Her tongue felt heavy, and her heart was literally falling out of her chest.

"Please say something," Jamie pleaded.

She wanted to say yes. She was about to get her mouth to cooperate to say the words she knew he was dying to hear, and then a thought came that halted her response.

"Oh, I don't know if that's such a good idea," she hesitated.

"Why?" he asked.

Cora couldn't answer. What could she say, that she was still thinking about her ex-husband and what he did to her? That she was afraid of commitments of this nature?"

"Tell you what; close your eyes."

Cora looked at him, confused.

"Close your eyes," he instructed once more.

Cora did as he said, closing her eyes.

"Now picture yourself walking on a beach alone; you're enjoying the smell of the sea breeze as it blows through your hair, the grains of sand are gently shifting as your feet sift through them; the more you walk, the closer you get to someone waiting for you at the end." Cora reveled in the imagery scene as she was transported to the very place he was describing. She could see the person taking shape, his features becoming more defined the closer she got to him. A broad smile broke out on her face as the euphoric feeling she felt in her chest warmed her body all over.

"When you finally make it to the end, who do you see?" he asked.

"You," she replied without hesitation. Immediately, her eyes flew open to meet Jamie's knowing ones staring back at her.

"I want you to take it as a sign to give this a chance," he spoke softly, an encouraging smile on his face.

As if mesmerized, she found herself nodding her head to say yes instead of verbalizing a no.

"Good, I will pick you up at eight," he returned happily. He straightened up.

Cora nodded in wonder, marveling at how he had managed to get her to say yes.

* * *

When Saturday night came, all the women in the house were anxious. Anxious because Cora was going on a date, and they all wanted her to enjoy herself, and they all wanted her to give Jamie a chance. Even Erin had given her her blessing.

"Mom, you deserve to be happy. Dad is all the way in Florida, living a new life even after he broke your heart and our family to create his new one. Jamie is a great guy, and I can see how much he cares for you, so if you were looking for an objection from me, you won't be getting any. Go enjoy yourself," Erin encouraged her.

Her daughter's blessing meant the most to her, so when Jamie finally knocked at the door, all she felt were the butterflies doing summersaults in her stomach.

The moment Jamie's eyes landed on her, she could tell he was floored. She had rendered him speechless.

"Wow, you look beautiful," he complimented with a wide smile, eyes glazed over.

Cora was in trouble. The butterflies had lodged in her throat now, making it hard for her to speak and reciprocate the compliments.

"Thank you," she breathed out. "You look really handsome."

Her sisters and her daughter exchanged knowing looks as their faces broke out in smiles.

"Now that you've both established how amazing you look, I have a piece of advice for you, Mr. Hillier," Andrea spoke seriously, though the light glint in her eyes betrayed her tone. "Take care of her and make sure she has fun. Don't come back here if she's not smiling by the end of the night," she warned.

"Yes, ma'am." Jamie grinned as he bowed.

The restaurant was lovely. It was close to the Oak Harbor Marina and looked very high-end. After being seated, their server came and started them off with a nice bottle of red cabernet. The conversation flowed, and Cora couldn't stop smiling at every word that came out of Jamie's mouth. It was refreshing to enjoy someone's company so wholeheartedly. She hadn't been on a date in so long. She and Joel had only attended social events together in the past couple of years, and even then, the focus had been more on the persons they were networking with than them having a good time as a couple.

Every time Jamie would stop to listen to her as she spoke, her face would get unusually warm under his unrelenting gaze. She felt like a teenager giddy from affecting the affections of someone she felt really strong feelings for.

After their dinner, they decided to walk along the boardwalk.

"Are you cold?" Jamie asked after noticing her slight shiver.

"Mm-hmm. A little."

Removing his jacket, he placed it over her shoulders. She couldn't help the seemingly permanently etched smile on her face.

Just as she was about to tell him that she was having a great time, her cell rang. Fishing it out of her purse, she put it to her ear without looking at the caller ID.

"Hello?"

"Hi, Cora, it's Joel."

Just like that, the high she was on just a moment ago instantly deflated.

"What do you want, Joel?" she asked, irritated.

Jamie stopped to watch her.

"I deserve that. I called because I never really apologized for what I did to you, and I wanted to say I'm sorry, Cora. I wish I could turn back time. I wouldn't have hurt you like that."

Cora sighed. "What do you want, Joel?" she asked once more, this time calmer.

"A second chance," he returned, getting straight to the point. "I miss you. I miss us. I want you back."

Cora's grip on the phone tightened as she closed her eyes.

"I'm afraid that is no longer possible, Joel. You made your choice, and now you'll have to live with it," she stated before removing the phone from her ear and ending the call.

On the ride back home, Cora barely said a word to Jamie, who kept throwing worried glances her way.

"Good night, Jamie. I had a great time." She smiled, but it barely touched her eyes.

"Cora," he started pleadingly. "You can't let him win. You can't let his words affect you like this. You deserve happiness, and the moment you're about to open up yourself to that happiness, he threatens to take it away. Please don't give him that power," he implored.

Cora gave him a small smile before heading inside. As she leaned against the door, her mind returned to Joel's request. She thought about the years she had spent with him and how that should count for something. She fiddled with the ring still on her finger. Her mind flashed to Jamie and how close she had grown to him and how he seemed to know just what she needed at any given time. Joel had never been like that. It had always been her trying to make him happy. He wanted a nice big house in the suburbs, and she agreed to move there. He wanted only two children, so they tried for only two. He wanted her to remain a full-time reporter so their income could maintain their lifestyle even though she had wanted to cut back — she did that for him too. For most of their marriage, she began to realize that it was her that had done everything to please him. Then Jamie came along, and he was teaching her how to love herself and put herself first. Why should she want to give that up?

Kimberly Thomas

Without any more hesitation, Cora removed the ring from her finger and placed it in her purse, ending that perceived happy life she once had and opening herself fully to the possibilities ahead of her.

She opened the door, intending to go after Jamie to see if he had already left. Jamie stood in front of her, hand raised as if ready to knock. His eyes registered his surprise.

"Jamie—"

Cora threw her arms around him and eagerly planted her lips against his, effectively rendering him speechless. When he got over the initial shock, he kissed her back with fervency.

When they finally came up for air, Jamie looked at her with hesitation in his eyes.

"What does this mean?" he asked.

"It means I'm saying yes to you, to me, and to my happiness."

Coming Next

Coming Next in the Oak Harbor Series

You can pre order Healing Hearts

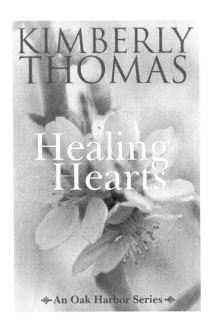

Other Books by Kimberly

The Archer Inn Series

Connect with Kimberly Thomas

Facebook
Newsletter
BookBub
Amazon

To receive exclusive updates from Kimberly, please sign up to be on her Newsletter!

CLICK HERE TO SUBSCRIBE

Printed in Great Britain
by Amazon

83303832R00113